TRIUMPH
ENTERTAINMENT
Division of Triumph Books
601 South LaSalle Street
Chicago, Illinois 60605

Credits

This book is not sponsored, endorsed by, or otherwise affiliated with any companies or the products featured in this book. This is not an official publication.

- Editor in Chief – Bill Gill, AKA "Pojo"
- Creative Director & Graphic Design – Jon Anderson
- Publisher – Bob Baker
- Contributors – Israel Quiroz, Jesse Zeller, Eric Gerson, Chris Schroeder, Richie Williams, Matt Farrell, Matthew Low, David Fashbinder

Copyright © 2003 by Triumph Books

If you can read, you can do anything!

Collectible Cards Games (CCG's) can be intimidating to beginners. And everyone who plays them was a beginner once. My first collectible card game was Magic: The Gathering in 1996. I remember seeing kids playing Magic in a driveway in my neighborhood. I grew up playing a game called Strat-O-Matic Baseball. It was the only strategy based card game out there when I was a kid. And Magic seemed like a tremendous improvement. I was dying to learn how to play!

I remember I was too embarrassed at first to ask for help. I didn't know where to start. What cards do I need? What score keeping devices do I need? How do I play?

So I bought a few Magic: The Gathering Books. (There were dozens of MTG strategy books for all levels of players, and from a variety of publishers). I read those books until I understood the game. I invested in some cards, and I built a deck.

Then, I finally got the nerve to go to a small tournament at a comic book store. I think there were about 16 people there playing. My goal that day: "Don't embarrass myself!" I wasn't worried about winning a single game. I was only worried about making an idiot of myself. But you know what? Those books really helped me out! They helped me so much that I actually took 2nd Place! And I just barely lost in the finals. My finals opponent wound up being a guy who became a good friend, and eventually helped me on Pojo.com. It was way cool!

I've played a few more CCG's since then: Pokemon, Yu-Gi-Oh and even Digimon (Man does that game suck!). Now I'm trying to get better at Dragon Ball Z. I was planning on reading a few Dragon Ball strategy books to help me. But guess what?! There aren't any!

How can a game like DBZ not have a book? It's one of the best selling CCG's out there, but no one's written a book to give tips to newbies! Well, it's time to change things.

Now I'm not nearly good enough at this game to write a book, but luckily I have friends in high places. I know a few people who are awesome at this game. And I recruited a handful of them to write articles to help beginners & intermediate players. I hope you find this book helps you understand the game more fully.

Hopefully someday I'll see you across the table. ;-)

Pojo

INSIDE *This Issue!*

Understanding DBZ

It is very easy to list the milestones achieved by Dragon Ball. The Japanese anime first appeared on television in 1986 and became one of the longest running animes in history. It was created by famed manga artist Akira Toriyama and produced by Toei Animation Co., Ltd. The series spans over 500 episodes and three series, and is the most popular anime in the world.

— BY ERIC GERSON

However, these few details barely scratch the surface of Dragon Ball's complex and colorful history. The storyline and the list of characters (even if one considers only the main characters) is so involved that an entire novel could be written about this animation series. We will attempt to condense the information into a few pages for "newbies" (the term for new fans of anime).

Dragon Ball revolves around the story of Son Gokou, simply called Goku in America, and the search for the mysterious and powerful dragon balls. The seven dragon balls are orange spheres

DRAGONBALL Z
Hero collection Dragonball Z series part 1.

with stars on them. The stars signify which number ball the person possesses. The dragon balls contain the power to grant any wish once the seven are brought together.

The series began as a Japanese comic called a manga. It told the story of a child named Goku, with a tail and funky hair. He also possessed a magic staff called the Niyoibo (or power pole) and the four star dragon ball. In the first comic, Goku meets Bulma, a sixteen year old girl who is searching for all seven dragon balls. She wants to wish for mountains of strawberries. Goku doesn't want to part with his dragon ball, because it was given to him by his late grandfather Gohan. Goku instead joins Bulma to search for the remaining balls.

As the story progresses, Goku encounters many more characters who join the search. He meets Oolong, a cowardly pig with the ability to shape shift; Yamcha, a desert bandit with amazing martial arts skills; Puar, a flying blue cat-like creature who can also shape shift; Umigame (or Sea Turtle), who introduces Goku to Master Roshi, who will become one of the most influential people in Goku's life.

Master Roshi is a hermit and a master of the Turtle Martial Arts. He is considered the strongest master on Earth. Roshi promises to train Goku when his journey is over, since Goku is the grandchild of Gohan.

As the group gathers the dragon balls, they encounter the first major villain of the series, Emperor Pilaf, who also wants to gather the balls to grant his wish. Instead of strawberries, Emperor Pilaf seeks world domination. Once all seven ball are finally gathered, the first wish to be granted by the dragon Shen Long is made by Oolong. He wishes for a pair of women's panties.

With their adventure over, Goku and the others depart, and Goku sets out to train with Master Roshi. Originally, this was to be the end of the Dragon Ball saga. Akira Toriyama only intended the Dragon Ball manga to be thirteen comics long. However, because of the success of the books, Toriyama continued the storyline. The story grew so popular that on February 16, 1986, the first anime episode debuted on Japanese television.

The story line continues where it left off, with Goku and his search for the dragon balls. After training with Master Roshi, Goku gains increased power and is joined by Krillin, a bald noseless monk who trains with Master Roshi so he can face the bullies at his previous school. The two become rivals and strive to be Master Roshi's only pupil.

However, since the students exhibit remarkable promise, Roshi decides to train both Goku and Krillin. When Goku's martial arts training begins, it is learned that his power exceeds that of an ordinary person. At this point, the Tenkaichi Budoukai became part of the storyline, which caused the popularity of the series to grow dramatically.

What is the Tenkaichi Budoukai and how is it pronounced? Tenkigh-chii Bah-doh-kigh is a world martial arts tournament where the strongest on Earth gather to compete. Master Roshi himself won the tournament years ago

and now uses the Budoukai as a way to test his student's powers and as a means for their training. To achieve this result, Master must enter the tournament in disguise. He uses the name Jackie Chun as his false identity (a play on the acclaimed movie actor and stunt artist Jackie Chan). Goku nearly wins the tournament, making it to the finals and facing Chun, but he ultimately loses.

The DBZ Storyline

The Dragon Ball storyline continues much in the same manner as before. Goku sets out to find the four star ball once more and encounters the Red Ribbon Army, a terrorist organization with global power. Goku gains remarkable strength as he battles the army and the assassins they send, eventually facing the entire army on his own and obliterating them. For the next three years, Goku trains for the next Budoukai.

When the Budoukai begins, two new main characters are introduced, Tenshinhan (Tien) and Chaozu. They are prize students of the Crane School. The Crane School is run by Master Roshi's previous friend and now rival, the Crane Master. Once

the Budoukai gets underway, it is apparent that Goku, Krillin, and Yamcha have grown amazingly in power, and that Tenshinhan and Chaozu are equal and in some cases, even more powerful. The final match between Goku and Tenshinhan ends with Goku barely losing, by hitting the ground first after slamming into a moving truck.

Impressed by Goku's power and realizing the evil ways of their previous master, Tenshinhan and Chaozu become friends with Goku and the gang. It is at this point that Dragon Ball's story becomes more complicated and interesting, thus transforming the series. The most powerful villain of the original Dragon Ball series is introduced – Piccolo Daimoa, the king of demons. He had been locked in a mafuba jar by Roshi's master (which cost him his life). Piccolo's is more powerful than the current fighters. To ensure that he isn't captured again, Piccolo sends his minions to kill all the Budoukai participants and eliminate the strongest fighters in the world. Further, Piccolo seeks the dragon balls to regain his youth.

With the help of Emperor Pilaf (he continues to make sporadic

appearances throughout the series), Piccolo gets his wish and kills Shen Long to prevent the dragon's power from ever being used against him. In the battles against Piccolo, Chaozu, Krillin, and even Master Roshi lose their lives, and Tenshinhan barely survives. It is only with incredible strength and persistence that Goku is able to defeat Piccolo. Before dying however, Piccolo lays an egg and is reincarnated.

Again, with Piccolo's death comes another change in the story. Goku meets Mr. Popo and Kami-Sama (God). Kami is Piccolo's better half. In return for defeating his evil side, Kami trains Goku. Goku studies under Kami for years until the next Budoukai and when Shen Long is reincarnated, he wishes his friends back to life. With his training complete, Goku competes in the next Budoukai as a grown teenager, along with the other participants who are older as well. The Budoukai is the last story of Dragon Ball series.

Piccolo

Piccolo, the reincarnation of his father, is fighting to avenge his father's death. Again, Goku (even with his new amazing power) is barely able to beat

Piccolo and finally wins a Budoukai. Further, it was at this point where he re-encounters Chi-Chi (she had been introduced early in the series). The two marry and Dragon Ball ends.

Dragon Ball Z

The Dragon Ball series contained 153 episodes and only ended as "Dragon Ball" in the anime form. The manga retained the name "Dragon Ball" and never changed its name to Dragon Ball Z. The new anime series, Dragon Ball Z, left most of the comedy and silliness of Dragon Ball behind to become a more dramatic action-oriented story.

In DBZ, Goku's true origins are revealed when he learns that he is from an alien race of blood thirsty warriors called Saiyans who destroy planets for money. With only four Saiyans, including Goku, still alive after their home planet is destroyed, Goku's brother Radditz seeks Goku out to join the survivors. He is disgusted that Goku has become human and has bore a half breed child, Son Gohan (named after his grandfather). Radditz steals Gohan and tries to force Goku to begin his mission to eradicate all life on Earth. Goku joins forces with his previous rival Piccolo, and both go to rescue his son. Piccolo kills both Radditz and Goku (who gives his life so that Piccolo can execute the final blow on Radditz). Piccolo adopts Gohan, who shows unbelievable powers when he's angry.

Once again, the story changes focus with the threat of the other two Saiyans, who are on their way to Earth. Goku, in Heaven, receives training from Kaio-sama (King Kai which translated means King of the Worlds). Other warriors train under Kami,

with Gohan learning from Piccolo. The fight with the other two Saiyans – Prince Vegeta and Nappa – costs most of the warriors their lives, including Yamcha, Chaozu, Tenshinhan, and even Piccolo. Krillin and Gohan only survive because they were able to stay alive long enough for Goku to show up.

With his power growing hundreds of times greater than before, Goku is able to defeat Nappa and Vegeta. The battle with Vegeta leaves Goku beaten severely and in the hospital. During the battle with the Saiyans, Piccolo and Kami's origins are revealed and you learn that they are Namekians, a race of peaceful but powerful aliens from the Planet Namek. Using Kami's ship, Bulma, Gohan, and Krillin set out to Planet Namek in search of the Namek dragon balls to wish their dead friends back to life.

On Namek, the warriors encounter the Saiyan's superiors and their leader, Freeza. Freeza's power is so great that even King Kai is afraid of him and warns Goku not to even attempt to engage Freeza in battle.

In the DBZ storyline, Vegeta wasn't supposed to make another appearance. But, since he was so popular with fans, Toriyama decided to incorporate him into the Freeza chapter. Vegeta kills most of Freeza's minions as all three groups search for the dragon balls, and Freeza kills most of the Namekians while he searches. As the battles wage on Planet Namek, Goku recovers with the help of senzu beans which are magic beans that completely heal those who ingest them.

With the help of Bulma's father, Dr. Briefs, the president of Capsule Corporation (the largest company on Earth), a spaceship is constructed from the pod that brought Goku to Earth. The ship also contains a gravity machine for training Goku. The gravity machine create conditions that are up to 100 times the force of the Earth's gravity. By training with the machine, Goku gains superior powers and defeats the strongest of Freeza's soldiers, the Ginyu Force, who had beaten and nearly killed Gohan, Krillin, and even Vegeta.

Battles

The battles with Freeza permanently change the fighting level of the series, as the warriors are forced to deal with an enemy who has multiple forms and a power level in the millions (Goku's fighting level when he was fighting Vegeta on Earth barely broke 20,000). With the death of Vegeta, the apparent death of Piccolo, and the merciless death of Krillin at the hands of Freeza, Goku undergoes a drastic power increase by means of transformation. Goku becomes one of the legendary Super Saiyan, a warrior who has the potential to gain power beyond that of anything else in the universe.

With his new power, Goku kills Freeza just as the Namekian planet blows up. During the battle, the Namek dragon balls and the Earth dragon balls are used to bring Piccolo, Kami, Vegeta, and all the dead Nameks back to life and to transport everyone

to Earth except Goku and Freeza.

The next chapter of DBZ, the Garlic Jr. episodes, were never part of the original storyline nor were they created by Toriyama. Toei produced them as a means to tie together the Freeza saga and the stories that follow. The appearance of Trunks in this series, the future son of Vegeta and Bulma, brings another twist to the already complicated saga. Trunks is a Super Saiyan from the future who kills Freeza and his father when they arrive on Earth to kill everyone as vengeance against Goku.

When Goku finally arrives back on Earth two years after his fight with Freeza, he learns who Trunks is and the terrible future he comes from. In Trunk's time, everyone has been killed by Androids built by Dr. Gero of the Red Ribbon Army. The few humans who survive live in constant fear and hiding. With his warning, Trunks returns back to the future and the Z warriors begin training to defeat the androids. When the androids finally show up, Goku barely survives the heart disease that Trunks had warned him about, and the warriors are no match for the androids.

During these battles, Piccolo reemerges with Kami and together become the Super Namek they once were in the past. However, an even bigger threat is introduced. Cell is an organic android created from the combined DNA of Freeza, King

Cold, Vegeta, Piccolo, and even Goku. Cell is from the future and has come to the past in order to absorb Androids 17 and 18, whom Trunks had destroyed in the future. If Cell is able to absorb Androids 17 and 18, he will be able to reach perfection.

As Cell searches for the androids, Goku recovers and takes Vegeta, Trunks, and Gohan to Kami's place to train in the Room of Spirit and Time (a Hyperbolic Time Chamber in the US). When they fight Cell, who does eventually absorb the androids, the Saiyans all reach a level beyond Super Saiyan. Gohan achieves the ultimate transformation that surpasses the Super Saiyan form. With his amazing power, Gohan obliterates Cell, but not before Goku again loses his life.

These storylines end the DBZ and Dragon Ball sagas in general, at least those created by Toriyama. The final villain of DBZ is the demon Majin Buu. "Majin" in Japanese means demon. He is released from a seal by Babidi, the son of Buu's creator. Buu's power is so great that nearly everyone dies at his hands, plus he is able to destroy the Earth.

During the Buu episodes, we are introduced to Son Goten, Goku's second child, Videl, Mr. Satan's daughter, and Super Saiyan 3, the final Super Saiyan transformation in the Dragon Ball manga.

With the help of Kaioshin (which when translated means "God of the King of the Worlds") and Kaioshin's ancestor, Goku is brought back to life. He is later joined by Vegeta, who Lord Enma (King Yama, the ruler of the afterlife, who decides who goes to Heaven or Hell) allowed to keep his body. And with the help of Mr. Satan (the world hero who took the credit for defeating Cell), Buu is defeated.

Just as Dragon Ball ended with a Budoukai, DBZ ends the same way. It takes place ten years after Buu's death. However, the main focus of the Budoukai is a child named Uub. Uub (or Oob) is the reincarnation of the evil Majin Buu who Goku defeated. Further, we are introduced to Pan, Videl and Gohan's daughter. Goku decides to train Uub and leaves his family once more. The two fly into the sky and Z ends.

Dragon Ball and Dragon Ball Z spanned 444 episodes, two TV specials, thirteen movies, and one OVA special. The manga consisted of 42 Tankuban, which are the volumes of books of the manga. By this time, Toriyama was done with Dragon Ball, but Toei Animation still wanted to cash in on DBZ's popularity.

They created Dragon Ball GT, which ran for 64 episodes and one TV Special.

Dragon Ball GT

GT's storyline takes place ten years after the end of DBZ and follows Goku, Trunks, and Pan who must search the universe for the dark star dragon balls. The dark stars were used by Pilaf to turn Goku into a child. If they are not gathered and the wish reversed within a year, the Earth will be destroyed. The series was not as successful as Z, since many of the characters were changed in unfavorable ways (Vegeta had shorter hair and a mustache) and the story returned to comic adventures like the original Dragon Ball.

Toei attempted to counter the silliness with the introduction of Bebi, the last Tsufurujin (the original race that lived on the Saiyan's home planet) and Super Android 17, a merger of the original Android 17 and an Android 17 created in Hell. The final villains of GT were the seven evil Shen Long dragons, who were created by an overload of negative energy in the dragon balls due to the abundance of wishes over the decades. Even with the action, GT could not survive and ended on November 19, 1997.

However, this was not the end of Dragon Ball. The three series had been translated and dubbed in various countries and came to America in 1995. FUNimation Productions Ltd.

obtained the rights to the first 13 episodes of Dragon Ball and released them on early morning television. The show wasn't very successful and was taken off the air soon thereafter. FUNimation attempted to introduce the series to the American public again in 1996 when they released the first 53 episodes of DBZ to FOX television. The show began to build a cult following but isn't still wasn't widely known until 1998 when Cartoon Network added DBZ to their Toonami line-up.

Since that time, the show has had a tremendous impact on American pop culture, with DBZ lunch boxes, shirts, blankets, and anything else that can fit a picture of Goku. The DBZ episodes will finish airing in Spring, 2003 and the Dragon Ball GT storyline will begin in Fall, 2003. The Dragon Ball saga will continue showing during the year, with the Piccolo Daimoa chapter airing this Fall along with the new GT episodes. ✪

Understanding the Dragon Ball Z
Collectible Card Game

– BY JESSE ZELLER

- *Card Types Explained:*
  - *MP's, Dragon Balls, Places, etc.*
- *Colors Explained:*
  - *Red, Blue, Orange, Saiyan,*
  - *Namekian, Black, Freestyle,*
  - *(Colorless)*
- *Playing Field*
- *Scouter, Z Sword*
- *How to win*

Card Types

What is the difference between a Dragon Ball and a Non-Combat? Can you stop a Physical Combat card with Trunks Energy Sphere? What in the world are these new Sensei cards? If you have been asking these questions, then all of your answers are soon going to be answered. Dragon Ball Z CCG has a barrage of different card types. In all, there are 10 different card types in DBZ CCG.

Physical Combat:

Physical Combat cards are the lifeblood of all physical based Beatdown decks. A deck that primarily focuses on physical Beatdown will have plenty of Physical Combat cards in their deck. This is because all physical attacks in this game are

"Physical Combat" cards. Remember, physical attacks will cost nothing to perform unless otherwise stated on the card.

But not only do you find most physical attacks being a Physical Combat card, you find that most cards that stop physical attacks being a Physical Combat card. They sort of go hand in hand, cards that perform physical attacks and cards that stop physical attacks are both labeled as Physical Combat cards.

You will find some cards that are neither physical attacks nor cards that stop physical attacks, but still have the Physical Combat label. They are still used at the time a physical attack is used. They are used in combat in place of an attack. An exam-ple of this is the card "Straining Rebirth Move."

Playing and using Physical Combat cards will happen most frequently in combat.

Energy Combat:

With Physical Combat cards being the lifeblood of physical based Beatdown decks, it is quite obvious that Energy Combat cards would be the lifeblood of energy based Beatdown decks.

The difference between Energy Combat and Physical Combat cards is quite simple. Energy Combat cards perform energy attacks or stop energy attacks. Unlike physical attacks, most energy attacks have a simple cost: two power stages. All energy attacks will cost two power stages to perform

unless otherwise stated on the card.

Like some Physical Combat cards, there are some Energy Combat cards that do not per-form energy attacks, nor stop energy attacks. These Energy Combat cards contain only sec-ondary effects and must be used during combat in place of an attack. An example of this is the card "Gohan's Nimbus Cloud." The beauty of these kinds of cards is that they cannot be stopped by the combat-killer, "Trunks Energy Sphere."

Playing and using Energy Combat cards will happen most frequently in combat.

Combat:

Like in any card game, there is a type of card that provides

support for your deck. In Pokemon, Trainer cards were the support cards for the deck. In Yu-Gi-Oh, Magic cards perform the same function. In Dragon Ball Z CCG, Combat cards provide the support for your deck.

Combat cards are composed of purely secondary effects. This means Combat cards do not perform attacks and only contain secondary effects. Combat cards are critical for many decks. Combat cards will give you the advantage by looking at your opponent's hand, or allowing you to draw more cards. Heck, there is even one Combat card, Dragon's Victory, which can win you the game. Most DBZ CCG decks will contain anywhere from 15-20 combat cards, and some contain up near 30!

Combat cards are very powerful. Because of this, you will find many cards that were made to fight Combat cards. In fact, most of these are Combat cards themselves! Piccolo's Fist Block will prevent your opponent from playing Combat cards for the remainder of the combat. Trunks Energy Sphere, considered the best card in the game by many players, stops the effects of any Combat card. Remember that these cards prevent your opponent from playing Combat cards. That means you cannot use Trunks Energy Sphere on a Physical Combat or Energy Combat card.

Playing and using Combat cards will happen most frequently in combat.

Non-Combat

Non-Combat cards are similar to Combat cards. Like Combat cards, Non-Combat cards do not perform attacks, and are entirely composed of secondary effects. The main difference is that Non-Combat cards must be placed into play during the "Non-Combat" step.

The Non-Combat step occurs immediately after you draw three cards at the beginning of your turn. Take a look at your hand. If any cards with the "Non-Combat" label are in your hand,

this is when you place them into play. You usually cannot use Non-Combat cards during this step though. The few exceptions are if they read "Use when needed" or "Use during the Non-Combat step."

Once a player enters combat, you are free to use Non-Combat card when the time arises. If the Non-Combat card is a defense, you use it when you would normally play defense cards. If the Non-Combat is not a defense, then you use it in place of an attack, just like Combat cards.

from player to player. Capturing a Dragon Ball is simple. You can use a card or effect that allows you to capture a Dragon Ball, or, perform an attack that successfully deals five or more life cards of damage. If your opponent takes five or more life cards of damage from a single attack, you may capture a Dragon Ball. When you capture a Dragon Ball, you have the option of using the Dragon Ball's power or not. If you use its power, you use it immediately. If you choose not to use the power, you cannot activate the power later, unless you recapture the Dragon Ball. Players may capture and recapture a single Dragon Ball between each other an unlimited amount of times per game.

Dragon Balls also follow a special Dragon Ball rule. Only cards that affect Dragon Balls can be used on Dragon Balls. That means that if a card said to "remove a Non-Combat card in play from the game", you cannot remove a Dragon Ball with the card because of two reasons. First, the card does not specifically state it can remove a Dragon Ball; and second, Dragon Balls are not Non-Combat cards! Another example of this rule applies to the card "Blue Terror". Blue Terror allows the user to search through their Life Deck for any card and place it in your hand. Even though Blue Terror reads "any card", it does not specifically state Dragon Ball cards, and therefore you cannot get a Dragon Ball card with Blue Terror.

Dragon Ball cards are played during the Non-Combat step. A

A special type of Non-Combat, known as drills, work similarly to Non-Combat cards. A drill is easily signified because the last word in the title of the card will be "Drill". Drills are Non-Combats that always have a constant effect. That means you do not need to activate the card to use its effects unless it says to. When you place a drill into play, the effects of the drill are immediate and constant.

Non-Combats are played during the Non-Combat step. Non-Combats are usually used during combat, in place of an attack.

Dragon Ball

Dragon Balls are not Non-Combat cards! Even though Dragon Ball cards have the "Non-Combat" label on them, they are not Non-Combat cards. The only reason they have the Non-Combat label is so that you know when to play them. Dragon Balls are played during the Non-Combat step. Another difference between Dragon Balls and Non-Combats is that when you play a Dragon Ball, the effects of the Dragon Ball occur immediately.

Dragon Balls can be captured

play from the game. You may search your Life Deck for any Battleground and place it in play." If a Location is in play, you cannot use this card. Run Away says to remove the current Battleground in play from the game, it does not mention Locations.

Battlegrounds or Locations are placed into play during the Non-Combat step. Both players benefit from the power of the Location or Battleground.

Personality

No DBZ CCG deck is complete without at least three of these cards. The Main Personality in a deck must contain at least a level one personality, level two personality, and level three personality. The personality card represents characters from the Dragon Ball Z world. Each personality comes with a unique power.

The personality you wish to base your deck around is known as your Main Personality. The level one personality is generally the weakest personality, with a weaker personality power compared to other levels of that personality. As you gain anger, and gain personality levels, your personality powers change and your power level usually increases.

You can also run additional personality cards in your deck, known as Allies. Like Dragon Balls and Non-Combats, allies are placed into play during the Non-Combat step. An ally's main purpose is to take a beating for the main personality or to dish out damage with their personality power. Allies cannot

Dragon Ball's power is immediately activated when played.

Battleground & Location

Battlegrounds and Locations are essentially the same thing. They are placed into play during the Non-Combat step. When you place them into play, you cannot declare combat against your opponent that turn. The effects from Battlegrounds and Locations work for both players, regardless of who placed the Battleground or Location into play.

So why are Battlegrounds called battlegrounds and Locations called locations? The rulebook states that Battlegrounds are where famous battles took place in the Dragon Ball Z world. Locations are famous places in the Dragon Ball Z world.

One common misconception about Battlegrounds and Locations is that when a card has an effect dealing with only Battlegrounds, the effects of that card will also work with Locations. This is not the case. The card "Run Away" states, "Remove one Battleground in

take over in combat unless the main personality is at zero power stages or one power stage above zero. Once that happens, any ally that you have in play can take over combat and is free to use their personality power. Another common misconception in DBZ CCG is that if an ally has a "Constant Combat Power", it does not need to take over combat to use their power. That is false. An ally still needs to take control of combat to use Constant Combat Powers.

An ally does not need to take control of combat if you redirect damage to them. To redirect damage, a successful physical attack that deals in power stages of damage must be performed against you. Then see how many power stages of damage it will do, and choose any one of your allies in play and have him take the power stages of damage instead of your main personality.

Allies are placed into play during the Non-Combat step. Allies can take over combat once your Main Personality reaches zero power stages, or one power stage above zero.

Mastery

Mastery cards were first introduced to the DBZ CCG during the Trunks Saga. Before the advent of Mastery cards, there was no reason to declare a Tokui-Waza. Gaining one additional PUR (power up rating) was not worth sacrificing good cards by declaring a Tokui-Waza. But the Trunks Saga arrived, and DBZ CCG players were given Mastery Cards.

Mastery cards are like a type of "super drill." Just like a drill, the effect a Mastery provides is always constant. Mastery cards cannot be removed or discarded from the game by any means.

To use a Mastery card, you must declare a Tokui-Waza. The Mastery card you are using must match the color of the Tokui-Waza you declared. You can only have one Mastery card per deck.

A Mastery card is placed into play at the beginning of the game. The effect a Mastery card provides is always constant.

Sensei

Sensei cards are a new concept to Dragon Ball Z CCG. They provided players with a small "Sensei deck", or sideboard. The twist is that only cards with "Sensei deck" or "Sensei deck only" can be used in the Sensei deck.

Sensei cards function somewhat like Mastery cards. They are placed into play at the beginning of the game. They cannot be discarded or removed from the game by any means. Sensei cards come with a small bonus. However, most of the Sensei's have effects that can be used only once per game.

Lastly, each Sensei card has a Sensei number on it. The number is used to signify the amount of cards you may have in your Sensei deck.

Sensei cards are placed into play at the beginning of the game. Most Sensei cards have a single effect that can be used only once per game.

Fighting Styles

In Dragon Ball Z CCG, there are six different fighting styles. The fighting styles are Red, Blue, Black, Orange, Namekian, Saiyan. Each fighting style has its own unique ability as well of a Mastery card to help you achieve victory.

Red

Defined as the aggressive style in the rulebook, the Red Style will focus on gaining anger while physically beating your opponent to the ground with a barrage of physical attacks.

Since the Saiyan Saga, many of the Red Style cards allowed you to gain anger. This is why the Red Style is so akin to winning by the Most Powerful Personality Victory. Aside from gaining anger, many Red Style attacks are also physical attacks. Red Style physical attack based decks got more powerful when the Red Style Mastery from the Cell Saga was released. The Cell Saga Red Style Mastery increased the power of your physical attacks anywhere from +1 power stage to +3 power stages of damage!

In the World Games Saga, a new type of Red Style arrived. The type that focused on energy attacks and lowering your opponent's anger. The exact opposite of what the Red Style was originally meant to be! Some players thought the change was for the better, and some

West Kai Sensei

156

7 POWER

Once per game during your "Attacker Attacks" phase, you may remove up to 2 Non-Combat cards in play from the game.

1 of 1
West Kai

©2002 Bird Studio/Shueisha, Toei Animation Licensed by FUNimation®. All Rights Reserved ©2002 Score

thought it was for the worst. Either way, the Red Style will always be remembered as the "anger style."

Blue

Defined as the calming style in the rulebook, the Blue Style works to battle against the Red Style by focusing on lowering your opponent's anger. The Blue Style also has an equal range of physical and energy attacks.

Like the Red Style, when people needed to fight anger, their deck was loaded with Blue Style cards. The majority of Blue Style cards lowered your opponent's anger. Many people did not start declaring a Blue Tokui-Waza until the Cell Saga. The Trunks Saga Blue Mastery was the most disappointing Mastery any player had ever seen. Because of this, Blue was very underplayed until the amazing power of the Cell Saga mastery.

Things changed for the better during the World Games saga. Everything was going in reverse as the World Games's Blue Style Mastery suggested that Blue try and win by anger! The Blue Mastery allowed all Blue Style energy attacks to gain anger, and do additional +1 life card of damage. This opened up a lot of new opportunities for the Blue Style.

Black

The Black style is the most powerful style in the game. The Black Style has some of the most incredible and powerful attacks in the game. It was no surprise that the Trunks Saga Mastery gave the Black Style a huge boost by allowing all Black Style attacks do +2 power stages and +2 life cards of damage.

Not only did the Black Style focus on powerful attacks, it focused on manipulation. If you are looking for a way to eat away at your opponent's Life Deck by removing individual cards at your leisure, then the Black Style is the best fit for doing that. Many Black Style attacks also force your opponent to discard a card at random from their hand, another aspect of manipulation.

Being the most diverse style in the game, players were intrigued to see what the new Black Style Masteries would bring. The new Black Style Masteries were not as powerful as their Trunks Saga counterparts, but they were still quite useful. Cell Saga focused on the usage of manipulation while the World Games mastery focused on Non-Combat removal.

Orange

The Orange Style is defined as the cosmic energy style. That is what Orange has always been good at, energy attacks. Both the Trunks Saga and Cell Saga Orange Style Mastery pushed the usage of Orange energy Beatdown based decks.

The Orange Style contains some of the most powerful energy attacks. Not only does the

This book is not sponsored, endorsed by, or otherwise affiliated with any of the companies or products featured in this book. This is not an official publication.

Orange Style focus on energy attacks, but it also has the best drills in the game. The Orange Style has the speed to get these powerful drills out. This is what makes the Orange Style such a dangerous foe.

But players wanted more. The Orange Style was slowly drifting away from powerful energy attacks and was starting to focus on physical attacks! Once again, the World Games saga switched up everything and focused on Orange physical based Beatdown decks by introducing an Orange Style Mastery which gave bonuses to physical attacks.

Saiyan

The Saiyan Style is the power style. It aims for raw, savage beatdown power, usually by the usage of physical attacks. A few Saiyan energy Beatdown decks do exist, but Saiyan physical beatdown is far more efficient.

All three Saiyan Style Masteries focused on one thing: card advantage. All three masteries allow you to draw at least one card when entering combat. But the Saiyan Style Mastery from the Trunks Saga was the Mastery to use for a physical onslaught. If you drew a Saiyan Style card when entering combat, your opponent would lose 4 power stages from their main personality, giving you a huge advantage for a physical beatdown.

As the Sagas progressed, the Saiyan Style grew more and more powerful; and it shows no signs of slowing down.

Namekian

The newest style, also known as the fluid motion style, is the Namekian Style. Like the Saiyan Style, the Namekian Style also focused on card advantage. In Dragon Ball Z, the Namekians were seen as quick and agile. The Namekians also had the ability to regenerate themselves. This aspect of Dragon Ball Z carries over into the card game. The Namekian Style has a large amount of cards that let you recycle cards from your discard pile back into your life deck.

Not only

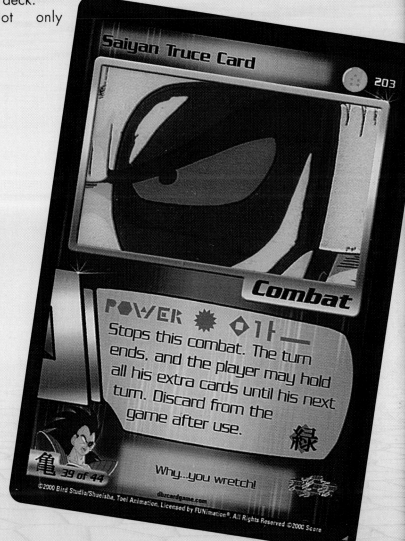

does the Namekian Style have many cards that regenerate your Life Deck, it has a huge amount of cards that power your main personality up to full. Physical beatdown decks have much trouble against Namekian decks because of Namekian's ability to power up so much.

Most Namekian decks will focus on the energy beatdown. The ability for Namekian to regain power stages tied in with the strength of many Namekian energy attacks leads most Namekian decks to aim for energy beatdown.

Equipment

The Scouter and Warrior Sword are two critical pieces of equipment to the Dragon Ball Z CCG. Both the Scouter and

103

Namekian Teamwork

Non-Combat

POWER Raise all of your Allies to their highest power stage. You may use all of their personality powers this Combat even if your Main Personality is at 2 power stages above 0 or higher. Discard 1 card from the top of your Life Deck for each Ally you have.

If we don't find the Android there's no telling what harm it might cause.

R R 16 of 19

Licensed by FUNimation® All Rights Reserved ©2001

DBZcardgame.com

Warrior Sword can be attained with the purchase of any starter deck.

The Scouter simply tracks what power stage a personality is at. It would be very hard to memorize what power stage you were at throughout the entire game. Instead of making the Scouter look dull, Score got creative and made it into the shape of the Z. To use a Scouter, simply place the Scouter on the right side of a personality, with the corresponding

DRAGONBALL Z

...ble Card Game

Discard Pile   **Life D...**

power level through the small cut out on the Scouter. Then slide the Scouter up and down the personality as you power up, or lose power stages.

If you place allies into play but don't have additional Scouters, you may take cards that are in your removed from game pile, and use them to track the power stages for an ally.

The Warrior Sword tracks the anger for a player. On each Warrior Sword are the numbers zero through five. A player's current anger level is displayed in the small opening at the bottom of the Warrior Sword. As the anger level increases, move the sheath of the anger sword up and the new anger level will be displayed in the opening.

Once a player reaches five anger, their Main Personality gains a level, and their anger is reset back to zero.

Playing Field –

Score gives you a simple playing field in Starter Decks. To be honest, most players don't use them once they become comfortable with game play. Use it at first to gain knowledge of game play, and where cards go. It's nice to have a Physical Attack Table handy as well. ✪

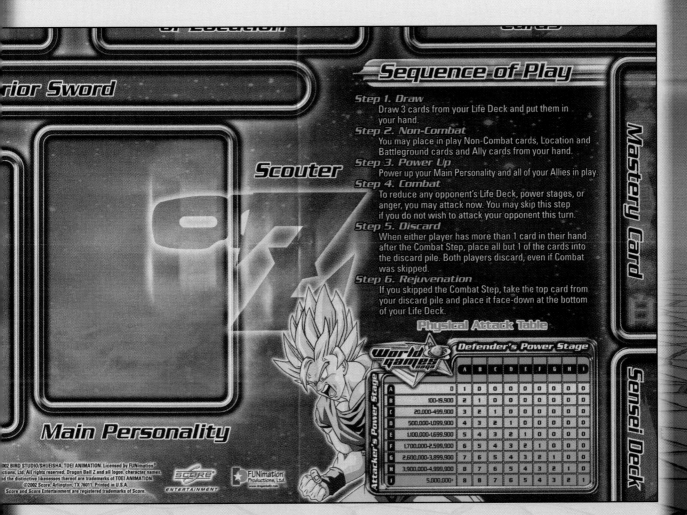

Sequence of Play

Step 1. Draw
Draw 3 cards from your Life Deck and put them in your hand.

Step 2. Non-Combat
You may place in play Non-Combat cards, Location and Battleground cards and Ally cards from your hand.

Step 3. Power Up
Power up your Main Personality and all of your Allies in play.

Step 4. Combat
To reduce any opponent's Life Deck, power stages, or anger, you may attack now. You may skip this step if you do not wish to attack your opponent this turn.

Step 5. Discard
When either player has more than 1 card in their hand after the Combat Step, place all but 1 of the cards into the discard pile. Both players discard, even if Combat was skipped.

Step 6. Rejuvenation
If you skipped the Combat Step, take the top card from your discard pile and place it face-down at the bottom of your Life Deck.

Physical Attack Table

Attacker's Power Stage		Defender's Power Stage								
		A	B	C	D	E	F	G	H	I
A	0	1	0	0	0	0	0	0	0	0
B	100-19,900	2	1	0	0	0	0	0	0	0
C	20,000-499,900	3	2	1	0	0	0	0	0	0
D	500,000-1,099,900	4	3	2	1	0	0	0	0	0
E	1,100,000-1,699,900	5	4	3	2	1	0	0	0	0
F	1,700,000-2,599,900	6	5	4	3	2	1	0	0	0
G	2,600,000-3,899,900	7	6	5	4	3	2	1	0	0
H	3,900,000-4,999,900	8	7	6	5	4	3	2	1	0
	5,000,000+	8	8	7	6	5	4	3	2	1

Warrior Sword

Scouter

Main Personality

Mastery Card

Sensei Deck

Dragon Ball Z CCG History

— By Israel Quiroz (IQ)

The Dragon Ball collectible card game (CCG) has been around for more than two years and has become one of the most popular card games today, but have you ever wondered how this game was created? What kept it alive? How did it become one of the largest and fastest growing games out there?

The Beginning.... a new game is born

At first, this CCG was just another card game. It had many flaws: 1) it was nearly impossible to play because the game was so complex; 2) the cards didn't look very good; and, 3) the cards were difficult to understand. These problems plagued the game in its early stages.

However, once the player base was able to decipher the rules, they also discovered some obvious weaknesses in the play. Multiple infinite loops were discovered that allowed most games to be won in less than 90 seconds. It became a matter of whoever got to go first, would most likely win.

Then there was the Trunks Saga...

The trunks Saga was the third set released. It contained a rulebook that was easier to understand than previous sets and new rules were developed to fix the major flaws in the game. This new set finally brought the game to life with better mechanics, understandable wording and brand new card types.

The Trunks Saga was what the initial Saiyan Saga should have been at the beginning. For the fans, the Trunks Saga became just what the game needed at the right time.

I went through a tough learning curve trying to learn the game when it was first released and it wasn't easy… to say the least.

A Voice is Heard

Once the Trunks Saga took hold, the game started to grow and there were more and more players who wanted to play and were teaching others to play. These new players started clamoring for official events and major tournaments, so they could test their skills against others.

Score heard the cries of the fans and developed a program that allowed stores to run sanctioned events, plus created a ranking system to encourage players to play in as many tournaments as possible. Once the system was perfected, SEVEN (Score Entertainment's Verified Events Network) was born. SEVEN is the system Score uses to keep track of each player's points, so their regional, national and international rating can be established. Kind of cool, isn't it?

Now that the player base had clear rules, better looking cards, and a ranking system that identified the best players. But they wanted more!

It seemed that the more incentives that Score developed for the Dragon Ball CCG players, the more they demanded. Score had developed a way to encourage the players to be competitive, but they wanted to put their new-found skills to the test. The over-riding question among the fans was who was the number one player in the World? They wanted Score to run a world tournament so they would know who owned the bragging rights and was the true world champ.

Let There be Worlds

The first official world's tournament was organized in [date], and the word spread that the best Dragon Ball CCG players would gather in Milwaukee, Wisconsin at the Gen Con Game Fair to determine who was the world's best player. The tournament offered great prizes for the winners, notoriety, and, at the end of the day, one player would hold the title of World Champion. The players had finally been given what they wanted and now it was time for Score to determine the format of the event.

After weeks of late night meetings and 34 _ devoured pizzas, the Score brain trust developed a format for this incredible event. They decided to make it a two-day competition. The first day would consist of 4 rounds of sealed deck and 4 rounds of constructed. Only the top 16 players at the end of the first day would earn the right to play on day two. However, the second day's format was kept secret. Once the top 16 players in the world had proven themselves, they would have to battle it out in a format for which they didn't have time to prepare. The secrecy surrounding the tournament play would allow the best player to rise to the occasion and emerge victorious.

Score's Intelligence Strikes Again

At the end of Day 1 of the world's tournament and after 8 long rounds of fierce combat, the top 16 players were ready to collapse. This was the moment when the brilliance of the Score plan was revealed. Each of the top 16 players were given a sealed booster box of Score's latest and unreleased Dragon Ball CCG set, the Androids Saga, which they would need to open up that night and play the following day. This slightly evil but ingenious format forced the players to adapt to a new environment, and put their deck building and metagaming skills to the test. By leveling the playing field among the top 16, it provided a clear and indisputable method to determine the true champion.

When Day 2 dawned, the top 16 players of the world arrived ready to duke it out. Some of them were worried and insecure about the decks they had created. Others feared that they had metagamed for the wrong environment. All looked like what they wanted but didn't have was some well-deserved sleep. Day 2 tournament play started and many different deck archetypes were seen. No two decks were the same and every deck was packing a few surprises of its own. No one knew what to expect from their opponents. Score's calculated format was working like a charm.

After several games, the stage was set for the final battle of the tournament between Aik T. and Brian Valdez. The stakes were high in this game because it would award one player with what every dragon ball CCG fan desired, while the other would be left with the knowledge and be reminded for months that he had come so close and had failed. With their egos on the line, both players sat down prepared to face their fate. After the dust settled on the first Dragon Ball CCG World Tournament, Aik T. was announced the first World Champion.

The End of Z

Score has been organizing more Dragon CCG major events since the first world's tournament, and the game now has a lot more to offer than it did in the beginning. With the Dragon Ball Z series nearing the end of its run on television, the players can only wonder what will happen to the game. In a recent press conference, Score has stated that just because there won't be anymore Dragon Ball Z episodes, that doesn't mean the game will meet its end. Score has the rights to make the Dragon Ball GT CCG. No one knows what the future will bring and one can only imagine what Score will do with the game. Questions abound, such as whether it be will possible to play characters like Raditz from the first Saiyan Saga set against characters like Pan and many others from the Dragon Ball GT series? Will Score go back and release sets based on the DBZ movies? The answers will come in due time. In the meantime, bear in mind that it is just a game and to have fun playing it. After all, that's what games are for, right? ✪

Cards You Can Buy To Get Started

You've seen your friends playing this Dragon Ball Z (DBZ) game and you want to be a part of the crowd, but you don't know where to start? That's what I'm here for. I'll help you get started, and in no time you'll be the guy to beat in your local area.

— BY ISRAEL QUIROZ (IQ)

Where to Start

If you've played any other Collectable Card Games (CCGs) or Trading Card Games (TCGs), you know the first thing to do is find a place where they sell the game and buy a starter deck. If you're brand new to CCGs and TCGs, you probably don't know what a starter deck is. Don't worry, we've all been there at one point or another.

I'd recommend that you ask one of your friends where you can buy one. Or, you can call your local comic book store and ask them if they carry the product you're looking for.

Dragon Ball Z starter decks can be found in many places and online, but I recommend you go to your local comic book shop because if they carry the product they may also run tournaments. If they do, it'll be easier for you to find someone willing to teach you how to play. If you can't find a comic book shop near you that carries the product, you'll have to go out and hunt one down. You'll

Saiyan Inspection

36

Non-Combat

POWER

Attach this card to your opponent's Main Personality. Your opponent may not use his Main Personality's personality power while this card is attached. Discard this card when your opponent places a Dragon Ball in play.

So these are the devices you androids use to rob people of their energy.

15 of 19
Vegeta

be looking for something called a starter Dragon Ball Z deck and they sell for about $10.99.

Once you locate a place where you can buy your starter deck, you'll have three or four different options to consider. You may want to get the most current game, which is the World Games Saga Starter Deck or the Majin Buu Saga Starter Deck. If you can't find either of those, than look for the Trunks Saga Starter Deck. No matter what you do, DO NOT buy the Saiyan Saga Starter Deck because the rulebook it comes with is old and very confusing.

After you get your hands on a starter deck you'll want to know how to play and this is where things can get a little frustrating. Read the rulebook and if you can't understand it, or if it's a little confusing, don't get frustrated and just fling it across the room. All players, even those who have been playing for years, need help with the rules once in awhile.

Score Entertainment (the company that makes the game) can help you here. They have an official website and a Message Board where they help you understand the rules and how to get started. If you have internet access, check out their website at www.dbzcardgame.com.

If you can't get online, then you need to find someone who knows how to play the game to show you how to play. Whatever happens, no matter how hard or frustrating, Goku never gives up and neither should you. Where there's a will, there's a way.

How do I Build a Good Deck?

Once you know how to play the game, you want to start building and testing your own decks. You need to find card spoilers from all the sets that have been released over the years. A spoiler is a document that contains information about each set. If you can get your hands on one, you'll be able to see what all the cards do in the game without having to go out and buy them.

The best place to find spoilers is at websites such as www.pojo.com. Review the spoilers from previous sets, and write down ideas about decks you'd like to try.

After your head is full of ideas and you feel the urge to build decks like a mad man, it's a good time to check out the Current Rulings Document (CRD) at Score Entertainment's website. The CRD has all the changes and clarifications that have been

Personality.

Physical attacks are better if your Main Personality has a low Power Up Rating (PUR) and high power stages because Physical attacks deal more damage depending on the strength of your Main Character. On the other hand, you have Energy attacks which aren't impacted by how strong your Main Personality is, but they do require you to have a high PUR or have a lot of cards that will gain you power stages.

After you've decided what type of attacks you're going to use, you need to find good cards that will keep you safe by stopping your opponent's attacks. Since this is your first deck, and you'll most likely be attacking your opponent, you'll need to have a lot of blocks and attacks in your deck. You'll want to keep applying pressure at every turn. I suggest you use from 25 to 30 blocks, and about 40 attacks. How many Physical and Energy blocks you play is up to you, but consider the following factors:

- Physical Beatdown Decks can usually handle Energy Beatdown Decks. If you can hit your opponent often, he won't have power stages for his attacks. You'll probably need more Physical Blocks in a Physical Beatdown Deck so you can have a good match up against Energy Attack Decks, and you'll want to protect your power stages so your attacks can deal more damage.

made to cards to help players understand the game better and to tone down some of the stronger cards to keep them from being abused.

The CRD is user friendly and can be found in the tournament section of Score Entertainment's website, look over it a few times and make sure the cards you want to use in your deck work the way you thought they did.

Building the Deck

By now you should have a list of the deck you want to build. Before you start putting it togeth-er, look over the following tips that'll teach you the basics of deck construction. Keep in mind that these are basic decks. You can step out of the boundaries set by these decks because each one is different. There is no formula for making a perfect deck.

Since this is your first deck, you'll want to build a Beatdown Deck. A Beatdown Deck tries to win by survival and is very aggressive. The first thing you need to do is to pick a Main Personality for you deck, and figure out what type of attacks work better with your Main

make. If specific decks give you trouble or you know your friends are using certain decks, you may want to consider Combat and Non-Combat cards that can hurt these decks or help you deal with them.

Now What Do I do?

After you've been playing and building decks for awhile, you may want to know what's the next step. Most players will find a place where they have leagues and tournaments and enter them. If you've only been playing with your friends or have only made decks on your own, I suggest you check out the tournament play without participating in it, so you get a feel for the environment and the type of decks being used.

After you've observed your opponents, and think you're up to the challenge, try playing in a league or with other tournament players. At the outset, play for fun so you can get used to new opponents before facing them in competition.

It's a lot better to play for fun and try new decks against each other, than to play in a tournament because highly-competitive players would rather win than have fun. At times, tournament play is not as fun as enjoying a good game. After you've gotten to some of the players on the circuit, sign up for a tournament and try your best. If something in your deck is not working, ask your new friends for their advice.

Try to hang out with some of the players before and after the tournaments. It is easier to meet new players in a friendly game

• On the other side of the coin, we have Energy Attack Decks that are a bit weak to Physical Beatdown Decks, but can usually handle other Energy Beatdown Decks. Most Energy Beatdown Decks need to use more Physical Blocks to stay alive. You'll want more Physical Blocks in a Energy Beatdown Deck, but remember that Energy Attack Decks can be very fast and running a low number of Energy Blocks can hurt you in the long run.

The thing to remember when building your deck is to keep in mind such factors as the type of power of your Main Personality. If your Main Personality can stop certain types of attacks, you can run less blocks of that type and more of others. Always try to figure out the weakness of your deck and try to add something to compensate when find yourself under attack.

Once we have our attacks and blocks, we can have fun with Non-Combat and Combat cards. How many you use and which ones you use will depend on the type of deck you're trying to

Cards You Can Buy to Get Started

than at a tournament match. I don't know why, but it works that way. Once you meet an experienced player who's been playing for a while and who's willing to help, show him your deck and ask him for suggestions. Ask him if there are any cards he thinks you should be playing and why he feels you should use those cards.

Experienced players have been around and generally know their stuff, but it's your deck and if you don't have make any of the suggested changes. After all, each player has his own style and no two play or think exactly alike. When you figure out what cards you might need for new decks or to improve your deck, try trading some of the stuff you don't need. You may also consider buying singles, because it works better than buying packs and hoping to get the one card you need.

I can't think of what else I can tell to get you started or for you to become the next Dragon Ball Z World Champion. The main thing is never forget that this is just a game. It doesn't matter whether it's the finals and the winner will get $5,000 or if it's

just a friendly match. I've seen friendships lost over games and that's a sad thing to see happen. Don't let your emotions get to you, and don't get frustrated when something doesn't work out as planned. Always respect your fellow players and be a good sport. Just because a player is rude to you, doesn't mean you have to be rude to them.

eeekkk.... I'm starting to sound like a grown-up now and we can't end it that way. It's time for me to wrap it up. Do your best and try to learn at least one thing from each game you lose. If you can do that one thing, it will be worth your while. Champions don't grow overnight and there will always be a new and stronger challenge waiting for you. Be ready and prepare yourself for an action-packed thrill ride. Oh, and make sure you have fun. After all, that's why you want to play this game in the first place. =)

Banned and Restricted *List*

Banned and restricted cards appear in every collectible card game. Some player figures out a way to abuse a card and ruins the way the game is supposed to be played. The creators of the game must then either ban or restrict the abusive cards. This keeps game play fair and fun.

As of the publishing of this book, the following cards have been banned or restricted from official tournaments by Score. The banned/restricted list is updated frequently. You should routinely check out Score's Official Website for the most up-to-date list on http://www.dbz-cardgame.com

Banned
The following cards are banned from all official DBZ CCG tournaments:

Dream Machine Battle
This Too Shall Pass
Dragons Glare
The Talking Ends Here
Chiaotzu's Psychic Halt.

Restricted List
The following cards are restricted and the text on each card should read: "Restricted to one per

deck." Thus, only one of these cards can be played in a tournament legal deck.

Blazing Anger

Enraged

Gohan's Anger

Vegeta's Smirk

Goku's Lucky Break.

Vegeta's Plans

Vegeta's Physical Stance

Nappa's Physical Resistance

Nappa's Energy Aura

Vegeta's Quickness Drill

Frieza's Force Bubble

Saiyan Truce Card

Trunk's Effortless Drill

Expectant Trunks

Straining Destruction Move

Blue Terror

Super Saiyan Effect

Battle Pausing

Teaching the Unteachable Forces Observation

Namekian Energy Focus

Initiative

The Official Tournament Rules from Score are nearly 50 pages long. If you are going to play in official tourneys, we highly recommend downloading, printing, reading and understanding these rules. You may want to keep your copy handy whenever you play in an official tourney as well.

Beginner's Guide to Deck Building

As you draw your three Dragon Ball Z cards to defend, your mind is racing. You need to win this game to guarantee a spot in the Top 64 at the World Championships. It's all or nothing. You've worked all year to get to this moment. But as you turn up your cards, your heart sinks. You realize these three cards will leave you with no defense, two worthless Non-Combats and an energy attack. You ask yourself "Why did I put this Non-Combat in here? It's useless for me!"

– BY JESSE ZELLER

You've made a critical error. And you might as well start packing your bags and making plans for next year, because your chance as World Champion is over.

An error such as this reflects on a fundamental concept of the Dragon Ball Z Collectible Card Game–deck building.

Deck building is the single most important aspect of the Dragon Ball Z card game. Where will you go in the game without a good deck by your side? When you build your deck, you should always be sure that it is a deck that you will be satisfied with, and a deck you will enjoy.

The question you need to ask is how you want to win a game of Dragon Ball Z. Currently, there are five ways to achieve victory:

- Survival

Survival victory, achieved through the use of "beatdown decks", is outlasting your opponent. You win by draining your opponent's life deck to 0 cards.

- Most Powerful Personality

A Most Powerful Personality victory is also known as "winning

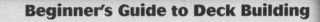

- Dragon's Victory

The second of the two "instant" victories. You achieve this victory by meeting the requirements on the Dragon's Victory card. Again, not recommended for rookie players.

Which one suits you best? New players should stick to Survival, Most Powerful Personality, or Dragon Ball victory strategies. Cosmic Backlash and Dragon's Victory should not be your first choice if you are a new player. Certain cards can directly remove Dragon's Victory and Cosmic Backlash from the game. This will leave you with no other chance at winning if

by anger." You achieve this victory by reaching your highest personality through the process of gaining anger.

- Dragon Ball

This victory is achieved by collecting all seven Dragon Balls of the same type.

- Cosmic Backlash

One of two "instant" victories. You achieve this victory be meeting the requirements on the Cosmic Backlash card. Not recommended for rookie players.

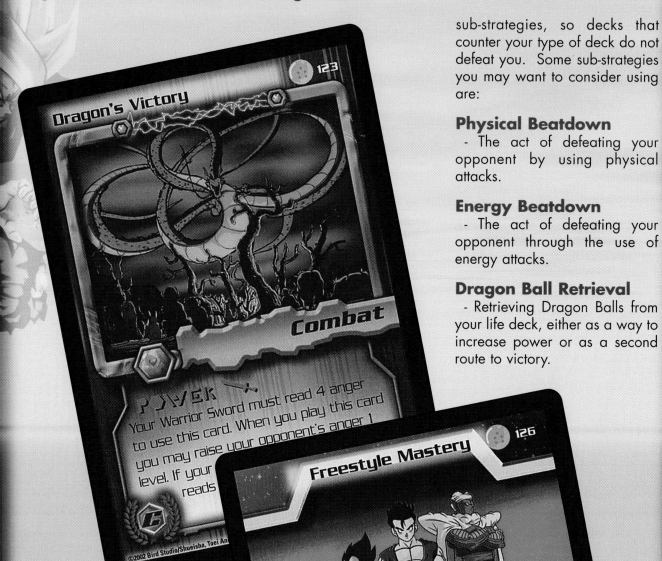

sub-strategies, so decks that counter your type of deck do not defeat you. Some sub-strategies you may want to consider using are:

Physical Beatdown
- The act of defeating your opponent by using physical attacks.

Energy Beatdown
- The act of defeating your opponent through the use of energy attacks.

Dragon Ball Retrieval
- Retrieving Dragon Balls from your life deck, either as a way to increase power or as a second route to victory.

Dragon's Victory or Cosmic Backlash were your main strategy. Even some veteran players will not try to win by Cosmic Backlash or Dragon's Victory because they don't consider them "true" victories.

Let's say you've decided to try to win by Survival or Most Powerful or Dragon Ball. You have now selected a main strategy. It's not a smart idea, however, to dedicate every single card in your deck to your main strategy. You need to develop further

Anti-Dragon Ball

- Countering Dragon Balls by stealing them or removing them from the playing area.

Anger Increasing

- Trying to gain anger, as a means to use higher personality powers or as a second avenue to victory.

Anti-Anger

- Fighting anger with multiple anti-anger cards.

Allies

- Using Allies for either beat-down or defense support.

Regeneration

- Regenerating cards from your discard pile back into your Life Deck.

Hand/Deck Manipulation

- Removing certain cards from your opponent's hand or life deck to destroy his game strategy.

You should try to use at least one sub-strategy along with your main strategy. This will give you more support to defend against many diverse deck types. For local tournaments, you should build your sub-strategies around countering the most popular deck types. This is called metagaming.

If Dragon Ball decks are popular at your tournaments, you may want to consider running anti-Dragon Ball cards such as The Power of the Dragon or Huh???. For premiere tournaments such as Regionals or Nationals, you should try and use a piece of each sub-strategy so you will be

prepared to battle against all decks.

Once you have decided how you want to win, and factored in any sub-strategies that you wish to include, it is time to decide if you want to declare a Tokui-Waza or not.

Declaring a Tokui-Waza means you can only use freestyle, named (which are freestyle cards), and cards that match the Tokui-Waza that you declared in your Life Deck. However, with this limitation comes great power. A great power in the form of a Mastery card. A

Mastery will supercharge your strategy to win the game.

Declaring a Tokui-Waza also gives you an additional one PUR for your Main Personality. Currently there are seven Tokui-Wazas that a player can declare: Red, Blue, Black, Orange, Saiyan, Namekian, and Freestyle. Obviously, there are some styles that will assist in certain victories more than others. For example, the Red and Blue styles are more likely to assist you in a Most Powerful Personality victory than a Saiyan

or Namekian style which are more likely to help a Survival win. Make your choice wisely if you plan to declare a Tokui-Waza.

A new mechanic to the Dragon Ball Z card game is the Sensei Deck. If you are familiar with Magic: The Gathering, a Sensei Deck is simply another name for a sideboard, with a few differences. You may use one of five Sensei cards, each of which comes with a unique power, dur-

ing the game.

However, each Sensei card has a Sensei Deck limit. The lowest Sensei Deck limit is one. The most is thirteen. There is one limitation with the Sensei Decks; you can only have "Sensei Deck" or "Sensei Deck only" cards in your Sensei Deck. If a card reads "Sensei Deck" on it, then you have the option to play it in your Sensei Deck or in your regular Life Deck.

One of the most common ques-

tions I am asked is, "How much defense should I run?" My response is always, "It depends." It depends on many factors. The most common factor is the popular deck type being used in your gaming area. If energy beatdown is popular in your area, you should run more energy defense. If you will be participating in premiere level tournament, the amount of defense your deck contains should be determined by how confident you are against other Survival decks.

In my last deck, I ran a meager 12 defensive cards. However, to make up for the small amount of defense, I had Allies in play to soak up most of the physical damage. If you were to run a deck with no Allies, then you'd certainly want to run more physical defense. One card you certainly do not want to leave out of your deck is Time Is A Warrior's Tool!

After you have a sufficient amount of defense, it is time to start working on what other cards you should include in your deck. Look at the different cards and ask yourself whether it will help you achieve victory. Just because a card is an Ultra-Rare, does not mean that it will improve your deck.

The most important three cards you need to have in your deck are three copies of Trunks Energy Sphere. This card is one of the few I would give a perfect rating. It also is the one card I tell all players to include in their decks. Trunks Energy Sphere is a great card because it stops combat cards, which are commonly used in competition.

You now have a big pile of cards from which you hope to build your deck. One aspect of Dragon Ball Z is that there is no finite size to your deck. You have the choice from 50 up to 85 cards in your deck. If you declare a Namekian Tokui-Waza, you may even want 90 cards!

The majority of beatdown decks being used today run around 85 cards. More commonly, you will see backlash and dragon ball decks aiming for 50 cards. They are going for a quick win. The backlash and dragon ball decks require a far greater reliance on certain cards, and thus need better odds for drawing a certain card.

Playing a namekian regeneration deck does not rely on certain cards, so it allows you to pack your deck to the full 90-card limit. If you want to balanced, or have no clue how many cards you should put in your deck, try sticking to 65-75 cards.

It's the moment of truth. You have your new and improved Dragon Ball Z deck ready to win a tournament. But before you even consider tournament play, you must do one thing—playtest!

Playtesting is the single most efficient way of improving and toning your skills with your Dragon Ball Z deck. Playtesting will reveal which decks are more powerful and the decks you can defeat with ease. Playtesting also shows if you are running too much defense or offense, non-combats, and other cards. If someone has a suggestion for how to improve your deck, you should always listen. It can never hurt to listen to another player's thoughts about how to improve your deck.

Once you have playtested different decks and recorded your thoughts about your deck's performance, it's time to tweak it. Tweaking a deck is simply making changes to it until you find the perfect synergy between the cards in your deck, and your playing style. One of the first things you should tweak is the balance between defensive and offensive cards in a deck.

Did you draw defense cards at the right time? Did you draw attack cards at the right time? Once you can answer "yes" to both questions, it's time to playtest again. If you are using an anger deck, is anti-anger giving you a problem? Are you gaining enough anger? Once you can balance these problems, you will need to wash, rinse, and repeat the steps of tweaking. If you follow these steps, you are on your way to becoming the next World Champion!

This is where the journey ends. I hope this article will help you in your endeavors on the path to greatness. Good luck and remember to playtest, playtest, playtest! ✪

Let a Player Play

How to Become a Better Player

Any card game that involves drawing cards from a randomized deck is going to involve a small amount of luck. Every once in a while, the better player will lose a match that should have been a victory. The poor or novice player will blame his many losses on "the luck of the draw" -- whether it be that his opponent received better hands or that he received lousy hands. How much of this has to do with deck construction? If you had a more consistent deck, shouldn't you get better draws? It is the conviction of the good player not to see luck as an enemy, but as an element of game play. In a sense, a good player will try to make his own luck and gather victories through skill.

— BY RICHIE WILLIAMS

This brings up the issue of winning versus losing. There is a great saying that you should worry about winning and not about losing. If you concentrate on maximizing the potential of your deck and utilize it in a way that decisively achieves its motives on the road to victory, then you are a good player. So, how does all of this relate to the game we all know and love, Dragon Ball Z?

First and foremost, DBZ is different from other games in the way that you can control the tempo of the game in clear cut, declared combats. Also, in DBZ there is less of a chance of "getting screwed" than in other games. In Magic, everyone fears the dreaded "mana screw" where you miss land drops and are unable to keep up with your opponent.

Let's take a game between a Blue deck and a Red deck from the Cell Games environment. The blue deck is a 50 card Earth Dragon Ball deck using Trunks HT as its main personality, up to

Caught Off Guard Drill

111

POWER

Non-Combat

Heroes only. When this Drill is placed in play, name a non-Dragon Ball card. That card cannot be played or used by either player while this Drill is in play.

2 of 6
Cell

Where is he?

©2002 Bird Studio/Shueisha, Toei Animation Licensed by FUNimation®. All Rights Reserved ©2002 Score

a level 5. It is running 3 Blue Leaving, 3 Nappa's Blinding Stare, 3 Dream Fighting, 3 Teaching the Unteachable Forces of Observation, 4 Trunks Energy Sphere, 3 Caught Off Guard Drill, 2 Winter Countryside, and other assorted goodies. The Red deck is Android 18 1-4. The purpose of the deck is to catch other top tier decks (probably also using Android 18) off guard by a quick 1-4 anger victory. However, the deck also has a strong element of beatdown with the level 2 being of the HT variety.

Finally, it has some utility cards such as Dragon's Victory (as a nice tech vs. another red deck or a surprise mode of victory), City in Turmoil, and Gohan's Kick. In most people's eyes, the Trunks Dragon Ball deck should have the upper edge. When looking at the match-up, you instantly notice that the Android 18 deck can't win by MPP. By nature, Dragon Ball decks are very defensive and quick. The Blue player should control the game by frequently ending combat, stealing the few earth balls his

opponent has, and keeping his opponent from using hurtful cards such as CIT or Gohan's kick.

Now, what does this have to do with luck? Well, let's say things go worst case scenario for the Blue deck and he starts to lose a game he shouldn't. The Red deck is able to drop a first turn CIT. The following combat, the Red deck enters combat with a Gohan's Kick and is able to take a considerable chunk out of the Blue player's deck. Things go from bad to worse when the red deck drops earth Dball's 4 and 5, making victory even more difficult for the blue deck. However, the good player will know that the Blue deck still has a good chance of winning. A good player will always keep his mind in the game and adopt the mentality that he refuses to lose and will find a way to win. This is difficult to envision, but true.

To better yourself as a player, there are many steps you must take. Sound deck building, a strong grasp of the rules, and dedicated play testing are all fundamentals. However, let's analyze further what separates a Scrub E. McJones from a Tim Batow or Brian Blanchard. Scrub may be a good player, with a very solid deck list that even a top player would be proud to use. So, what separates him from being great instead of just good? First, he may not have the outlook of a great player. He may be confident in his playing skills, but he will not go into every match thinking that he has a better chance to win the game than his opponent. Like many other players, he may not view the game as something that he can control or dictate the style of play.

Let's go back to the idea of "getting screwed." Sure, your opponent could enter combat against you and you could draw 3 non-combats, but unless your deck is 50% non-combats that outcome is very unlikely. Deciding how to compose your deck of the perfect amount of defense, offense, tech, etc. is a very tricky ordeal. While you might throw a stack of cards together and dominate your local scene, if you continue that approach you won't be able to compete on a larger scale.

If you wish to become a better player, card choice plays a big role. If you have been playing the game for a while, chances are you already make good card choices and don't really need this advice. However, a newer player who wants to improve really needs to make intelligent card choices. Each slot in your deck is valuable, and must serve a defining purpose.

Sure, that Smokescreen or Prepared dodge may look awe-some to someone just starting out, but over time you realize that they do not deserve a slot in your deck. Before this turns into a deck building clinic, just realize that finding the balance of

offense, defense, or whatever you are trying to accomplish, can only come through play testing.

Let me close by providing you with the winning player's mantra. You are going to lose games, no doubt about it. Again, you should only worry about the games that you win. To improve yourself as a player, you have to throw out the idea of luck in the game and analyze how and why you lost, and what you can do to keep it from happening next time. If you consistently lose to a 1-5 anger deck, it is up to you to decide if it is worth using card slots as anti anger.

How many anger decks won a regional or placed high in the last National or World Competitions? Not many. If you are consistently losing to Dragon Ball victory, then you must tech, tech, and tech some more. But, then again you may over-tech and draw useless cards in a match against a non-Dragon Ball deck! As you can see, you must find a balance that suits your style of play. Each loss should be an experience that can

only make you stronger.

I can think of many games where I have been beaten badly. I can think of many games where my defeat was one-sided. However, never once have I been completely dominated. Any given deck can have a terrible match-up, but it is up to the player to compete at the highest level possible for the given game. You can fight a losing battle valiantly, and once in a while you will come out on a top of a game that your deck should not have won.

As a final note, don't forget that this is a game. Yes, that means you should have fun while play-

ing it! For some competitors, they may only have fun when they win. For those who fall into that category, by all means take every step necessary to put forth what you feel is the deck that has the best chance to win.

For other players, having fun means using their favorite DBZ character, even if they are useless in the CCG. Other people are going to play certain cards in their deck because they like the picture. I take my hat off to those who can enjoy themselves by playing specific cards because they like them, not because they are viewed as

"good."

I hope that all players – no matter how seriously competitive or simply fun-loving – can draw something of value from this article and max out their potential, regardless of their approach or views on the game. ✪

Killer Deck
Majin Vegeta's Mayhem

— BY CHRIS SCHROEDER

Majin Vegeta is one of the new personalities introduced in the Babidi Saga set, and this card is both powerful in terms of power stages and personality powers. However, Majin Vegeta didn't get the best level 1's from the Babidi Saga. The Preview 7 from the World Games Saga will be the number one card to play in any Majin Vegeta deck. Its power has so many effects, which include discarding all Allies in play.

For this Killer Deck report, I am going to share a deck that I made after the release of the Babidi Saga. It's based on Majin Vegeta and the Red Style Mastery from the Cell Saga. This style gives physical attacks +3 power stages, along with cards that do an insane amount of damage. Moreover,

after all that, you still get the base damage.

This is a physical beatdown deck. There are not a lot of Non-combats I would use besides the eight found in this deck. One comes out at the beginning of the game, and the other two are Dragon Balls. With City in Turmoil in play, it doesn't hurt the deck.

However, there are a few Non-combats you can't leave out, such as Expectant Trunks and Frieza is Ready. The Dragon Balls are useful because Namek Ball 4 discards all Non-combats in play. Also, Namek Ball 7 can steal a Dragon Ball and with this

out, Red Resistance can now target three Non-combats in play and remove them from the game after stopping an energy attack.

All the physical attacks in this deck cause a lot of damage. The Majin Knee Strikes do +7, and with the Red Master they will do +10, and most often knock your opponent to 0. Red Double Strike, Red Shattering Leap, and Majin Vegeta's Frantic Attack are attacks that can stay in play for one more use.

The Red Tilted Punch requires your opponent to use a Combat card before you use that attack, so it may stay in play for two more uses. It also does +3 or more depending on the mastery. With so many attacks and high power levels, you can overwhelm your opponent easily if they don't stop all physicals or end combat.

Gohan's Kick is essential to overwhelm your opponent in 1 combat. It locks your opponent into combat and they can't stop your physical attacks for the whole combat. There are also some red essential cards like Red Overbearing Attack and Red Back Kick that are good and worth using.

Trunks Swiftly Moving and Pikkons Leg Catch are great blocks that have excellent secondary effects. One gives you another physical attack and the other powers you to full and allows you to shuffle back the bottom 3 cards of your discard pile into your life deck.

Red Resistance is one of the new Babidi Saga cards that has an amazing effect. Its ability to remove up to three Non-combats in the play from the game works well against orange decks and all of their drills. To be successful, you have to make sure to get Namek Ball 7 into play.

The rest of the blocks are used for anger and the other red cards are there so that the mastery will do +3 power stages every combat. Majin's Perfect Defense is also perfect for Majins.

The energy attacks in this deck are Red Energy Blast and Vegeta's Jolting Slash. The first one is used to kill off an Ally or drill and the other is to stop all physical attacks performed against villains. Against Heroes, this deck is great, but against Villains, it's a little more tricky.

Finally, let's look at the Combat cards that are being used in the current tournament environment. Trunks Energy Sphere is a staple. Android 18's Staredown is great for knocking out Omni Blocks or even regular blocks from opponent's hands leaving them vulnerable.

For defense against allies, Cells Presence gets the job done by removing all Allies in play from the game. Red King Cold Observation is another defense against Allies as well. It also gets rid of all Non-combat cards in play as well and raises your anger 1.

Evil's True Face and Majin Quickness are very good in

Majin decks as well. Evil's True Face gives an extra boost for your physicals. It adds another +3 power stages to your physicals, plus you get to draw a card.

Majin Quickness allows you to draw two cards when your opponent uses an effect that lets him draw a card. This card can help you keep up with Saiyan decks,

since they provide your opponent a massive card advantage. ✪

Main Personality: 5

Majin Vegeta, The Dark Prince (WGS)

Majin Vegeta, The Evil (BS)

Majin Vegeta, Uncontrollable (BS)

Majin Vegeta, The Malicious (BS)

Majin Vegeta, The Malevolent (BS)

Mastery/Sensei: 2

Red Style Mastery (CS)

North Kai Sensei [13] (WGS)

Side Deck: 9

Huh???

Breakthrough Drill x3

Red Sniping Shot x3

Goku's Blinding Strike x2

Non-Combats: 8

Victorious Drill

Where there's life there's hope

Fatherly Advice

Expectant Trunks

Frieza is Ready

Vegeta's Quickness Drill

Namek Dragonball 4

Namek Dragonball 7

Location/Battleground: 3

City in Turmoil x3

Physical Combat: 41

Majin Knee Strike x3

Majin Vegeta's Frantic Attack x4

Gohan's Kick x3

Red Tilted Punch x2

Red Overbearing Attack x3

Red Back Kick x2

Red Shattering Leap x3

Red Energy Defensive Stance x3

Red Resistance x3

Red Shifty Maneuver x2

Red Blocking Hand x3

Pikkon's Leg Catch x3

Nappa's Physical Resistance

Majin's Perfect Defense x3

Trunk's Swiftly Moving x3

Energy Combat: 7

Vegeta's Jolting Slash x3

Red Energy Blast x2

Nappa's Energy Aura

Frieza's Force Bubble

Combat: 19

Red Double Strike x2

Red King Cold Observation

Trunk's Energy Sphere x3

Android 18's Staredown x3

Cell's Presence x2

Cell's Threatening Position

Time is a warriors tool

Super Saiyan Effect

Majin Quickness x2

Evil's True Face x3

Killer Deck
Dakrillin

Orange Eye Beam
Energy Combat
Energy attack doing 5 life cards of damage. Costs 3 power stages to perform. If you declared Tokui-Waza, this attack does 7 life cards of damage instead.
I will clear the area.

— By Jacob Lackner (Dakrillin)

This is a standard play deck that wins by survival. It quickly slings those Non-Combat cards on the table with cards like Tien's Block and Orange Searching Maneuver. These drills usually power up the energy attacks to do massive amounts of damage, but many also protect you from your opponent's attacks. There is even one that is used to get rid of your Opponent's pesky Non-Combat cards that destroy your Non-Combat cards.(Orange Destruction Drill).

MP's

I decided to use Android 19 because all of his powers read "If you declared an orange tokui waza…" Orange is already really short on Energy defense, and Android 19's level 1 power will help you with that. This deck doesn't really want to gain anger, since when you level-up, you destroy your non-combats (wouldn't want that would we?). Another reason is because you really want to stay at level 1 to protect yourself from ener-

gy attacks. If you know you're going up against a physical attack, don't worry about raising your anger, because the level 2 power will be of much more use. To decide on which cards to use in my sensei, I first took a look at what type of decks were winning, and they were Dragon Ball decks. So I threw the card "Huh??" in. I also threw in two copies of Goku's Blinding Strike, since, it's not only a powerful 7 life card energy attack, but it also allows you to choose 3 cards in your opponents

Life Deck and discard them, fun ..isn't it?

Masteries & Sensei

I decided to use the Orange Style Mastery from the Trunks Saga, since it makes your energy attacks cheaper, and causes them to inflict more damage. I didn't use the CS one because your energy attacks will cost 2 power stages, and this deck already has a good deal of physical defenses.

I decided to use the East Kai sensei, since you really want to be at your highest power stage to inflict the greatest amount of energy beatdown, but this sensei can only be used once in the entire game, so you may want to use it when you know your opponent is going to deliver a massive amount of physical beatdown to your life deck.

Energy Combat

To decide on which energy combat cards to use use, I decided the minimum amount of damage I wanted them to deal (before modifiers) was 5 life cards, as I want to deliver the largest amount of energy beatdown possible, in one combat. I included only two energy combat cards that stopped energy attacks, since there aren't many to begin with. I also include Power Boost, since it adds an additional 2 life cards to an energy attack, and makes it free! Since Android 19 uniquely has 13 power stages, I decided to include Orange Special

Beam Cannon, with power boost this will do a minimum of 16 life cards, and this is with out any drills!

Since this deck is mainly energy beatdown, I decided that I wouldn't include very many physical combat cards other than defenses. I did include a

few, though. I put Hidden Power Level in so that I could get to my maximum power stage when I needed to. I have Orange Searching Maneuver in this deck, since it can fetch me two drills from my deck and place them into play at the beginning of the next Non-Combat phase. The only other Physical attack in this deck is Orange Uppercut, and I've included this card because it is not only a decent physical attack, but if, in addition you pay 2 power stages you may search your Life Deck for any one energy combat card and place it in your hand! Need to finish the game? Pull out Orange Scatter shot. Need to deliver an unstoppable Energy Attack? Pull out Krillin's Heat Seaking Blast!

Drills

I knew I would include Android Attack drill, since you can have up to 3 of these out at one time and each will inflict an additional 2 life cards of damage. I also include Orange Aura Drill, because it can also power up my energy attacks. I also decided to use Orange Energy Dan Drill (a remarkable card). It, in a sense, inflicts one extra life card of damage to one of your energy attacks in a combat, BUT it also allows you to decide WHICH card in your opponents ENTIRE Life Deck will be discarded!

I included Severe Bruises and Awful Abrasions since this is a standard play deck, and it allows me to not only lower my opponents anger to 0, it also allows you to keep it there, until they fulfill what is stated on the card! The last thing I did was decide which Combat Cards to use, I only include two in this entire deck;

Assault and Battery (Operated)

Main Personality (3)
1x Android 19 (CS)
1x Android 19, Recalled (CS)
1x Android 19, Recharged (CS)

Mastery (1)
1x Orange Style Mastery (TS)

Sensei Deck (3)
1x North Kai Sensei (WGS)
2x Goku's Blinding Strike (WGS)
1x Huh?? (IR Promo)

Energy Combat (39)
2x Orange Power Ball (AS)
3x Orange Kamehameha Attack (CS)
1x Good Advice (FS)
3x Orange Focused Attack (CGS)
3x Orange Eye Beam (AS)
2x Orange Energy Shot (CGS)
2x Orange Focused Blast (CS)
3x Power Boost (CGS)
3x Orange Energy Discharge (CS)
3x Orange Special Beam Cannon (TS)
2x Orange Planet Destruction (FS)
3x Krillin's Heat Seaking Blast (TS)
2x Orange Goku's Kamehameha (CS)
2x Orange City Destruction (AS)

2x Orange Energy Setup (CGS)
2x Orange Scatter Shot (CCPP)
2x Orange Energy Deflection (CS)

Physical Combat (16)
3x Orange Searching Maneuver (CS)
2x Hidden Power Level (SS)
3x Orange Fist Catch (AS)
2x Orange Left Kick (CS)
2x Orange Deflection (CS)
2x Tien's Block (CGS)
2x Orange Uppercut (AS)

Combat Cards (2)
3x Trunks Energy Sphere (TS)

Non-Combats (23)
3x Orange Aura Drill (AS)
2x Orange Steady Drill (CGS)
2x Orange Burning Aura Drill
2x Orange Power Stance (WGS)
1x Orange Destruction Drill (FS)
2x Orange Gaze (CS)
1x Awful Abrasion (CS)
2x Sever Bruises (AS)
3x Android Attack Drill (AS)
1x Senzu Effect (CS)
3x Orange Energy Dan Drill (SS)
1x Orange Halting Drill (CS)

Two copies of Trunks Energy Sphere. I include this card for pretty much one reason: Black Searching Technique (BST). BST can allow your opponent to be rid of all of your Android Attack Drills, and we really dont want this to happen! If you

aren't playing a Black Deck to use it on, got for other Stuff like Smokescreen or Prepared Dodge, so that your opponent will take the damage they are trying to not take! ✪

Killer Deck
Cell Namekian

— BY RICHIE WILLIAMS

Babidi Saga was recently unleashed on the masses, and its impact is already being felt on the tournament scene. Goku's Colorless Anger is the newest bundle of brokenness, but it's slowly being corrected. A lot of new cards were introduced for different styles to utilize, but certain deck archetypes remain entrenched in power.

One such deck is Namekian, which received a whopping total of one new card in the set. For this article, we'll focus on the deck used by Tim Batow & I to win our respective regionals. It is a very finely tuned machine, capable of dealing with most popular decks in the environment.

There are few metagame changes needed for the new environment, such as increasing the total number of Pikkon's Leg Catches to three to deal with the influx of Majin Vegeta decks. Let's get started by examining the modified deck:

At first glance, this seems like a somewhat unorthodox deck with odd card choices. I will go through the list section by section in order to explain the deck and why certain cards were included. It is a complex deck, but with time and practice you will be well equipped to handle whatever your opponent brings to the table.

The main personality in the deck is Cell. The reason, of course, is because he is A) Namekian and B) can't be stunned like Piccolo can. Contrary to popular belief, Cell's strength is NOT the fact that he can run Cell's Style. In fact, two may even be too many for this deck.

This deck was originally Piccolo the Trained, and evolved to a Cell deck with minor modifications to avoid being stunned. He has other subtle advantages, including a useful power, high power-up rating, ability to start at full versus many characters, etc.

The Trunks Saga Mastery is the obvious choice for this deck. There are many ways to manipulate the discard pile in order to re-draw the power cards and powering up to full is key for an energy deck. The North Kai Sensei is useful for both its large Sensei Deck size and ability to turn a mirror match in your favor.

The Sensei Deck contains mainly Anti-Dragonball deck cards, with the three Goku's Blinding Strikes in nearly every game and the Namekian Knee Strikes used versus heavy ally decks that easily get to zero. Breakthrough drills should only be used versus Earth Ball decks, not Dende.

Conversely, Hero's Drill and Namekian Offenses should be sided in versus Dende Ball decks. The things to look for to help tip you off on whether or not your opponent is playing a Dragon Ball deck is deck size, Blue Style Mastery (CS), and Trunks HT or Master Roshi Main Personalities. If you don't already know which kind of balls they are using, side in Breakthrough Drills along with Huh??? as a rule of thumb.

The defense is slim, if nothing else. However, this doesn't mean that the deck will be taking massive damage every turn. It is a very intricate defense that requires strategic blocking/conservation of stages. The four dual blocks (three Goku's Super Saiyan Blast and one Yamcha's Skillful Defense) can be mixed and matched, as long as there are a total of four.

Running 2/2 or 3/1 can often fool your opponent into thinking you play more defense than you actually do, and he may assume

you are playing full sets of each card to be in your deck. The lone Namekian Energy Catch is in the deck because it's a pure energy block that stops focused attacks. Also, it is Namekian.

With your mastery and Namekian Energy Focuses requiring the bottom card of your discard pile to be Namekian, always use that style of card over a colorless alternative. This rule is why we use three copies of Namekian Ducking Technique as opposed to two of the more powerful Pikkon's Leg Catch.

The Non-combats in this deck are vital to its function. One may question the use of CIT with such powerful non-combats in the deck, but I will explain later.

Foreboding Evidence and Frieza is Ready are great stallers that will always give you a net gain of life cards unless your opponent removes them quickly.

Foreboding Evidence has an obvious synergy with the great amount of Combat cards in the deck. The drills provide ridiculous card advantage. Since Namekian manipulates its discard pile so easily, Vegeta's Quickness Drill is more powerful in this style than any other. It essentially doubles the effect of your mastery.

Expectant Trunks and Fatherly Advice are staples, grabbing a useful card for the situation. However, the real MVPs of the deck are Krillin's Concentration and Piccolo And Heroes Gather. These cards are so valuable in Namekian that it is crazy not to run three copies of each. They are so versatile, that their usefulness is unlimited.

With these two cards, you can grab Namekian's Strike, which will lead to getting a nice attack such as Namekian Quick Blast or Goku's Blinding Strike. Also, Super Saiyan Effect

or Time is a Warrior's Tool can be grabbed if you must go on the defensive. Android 18's Stare Down can incapacitate your opponent's defenses while you unleash three or four devastating energy attacks in a row.

We haven't even mentioned that single tech cards, such as Cell's Presence or Cell's Threatening Position, can be taken depending on the style of deck you are playing against. Using Android 17 Smirks and Stupid Tricks! will further the versatility of these non combats.

The Combat card searchers also bring great value to the deck. For example, a Piccolo and Heroes Gather can turn the tide of the game in your favor. If you are holding an Android 18's Stare Down in your hand from last turn. Your opponent declares

combat, and you draw a Namekian Quick Blast (that you had set up earlier in the game) from the bottom of your discard pile for your mastery. You draw three cards, two of which are ineffective for the situation (lets say a Non combat and a Cell's Threatening Position) and the other is a defense.

On your first phase, you play Android 18's Stare Down, removing the card from your opponent's hand that proves the biggest threat. It may or may not be a defense. After the middle phase of combat when it is winding down toward the end of the battle, you begin to go to work. It's time to activate Piccolo and Heroes Gather. In this example, assume the bottom card of your discard pile is Namekian. If it wasn't, you could always get a Namekian's Strike to get Namekian Quick Blast and clean up the discard pile.

For this scenario, we'll say the bottom card is Namekian Focused Blast. It allows you to grab Namekian Energy Focus. Depending on whether or not you thought/knew if your opponent has another defense, you could get an Android 18's Stare Down. If you want to go for the jugular, you could get a Namekian's Strike.

If you needed more stages, you could get an Aura Clash to level up. Since you already played a Stare Down earlier this combat and know your opponent has no more defenses, you should get a Namekian Energy Focus and Namekian's Strike with the Piccolo and Heroes Gather. Use Namekian Energy Focus for the bottom card, being that it is an

energy doing 5.

Search your deck for Goku's Blinding Strike. Namekian strike for 4, and get Goku's Blinding Strike. Focused Blast for 5. Goku's Blinding Strike for 7, name three. As you can see, there are a number of options to decide how to dismantle the opponent from just one Piccolo and Heroes Gather. The more you play and become familiar with your deck, the better you will know what cards you need in which situations.

The location control in this deck is unlike any I have ever played. As you can see from the above example, it is very easy to get a Namekian Strike or Namekian Energy focus into your hand, both of which allow you to search your deck for an energy combat card. Gohan's Nimbus Cloud is an energy combat card you can grab, so you can pull out Planet Vegeta.

Planet Vegeta is in the deck only because it is a location. It doesn't help you, but it doesn't help your opponent either. City

in Turmoil can also be put into play using Cell's Instant Transmission. As you can see, the ability of the deck to pull Combat cards with ease is vital to its overall control of the game.

While Planet Vegeta should be put into play for the sole purpose of removing your opponent's location, City in Turmoil should be used with much more caution. Evaluate the situation very carefully and determine the immediate and long term effects. If your opponent has a Frieza is Ready in play and you plan on dealing enough damage in the near future to effectively take an insurmountable lead, it is wise to get a City in Turmoil in play as quickly as possible.

Always be sure to take into account which Non-combats you still have in your deck. Determine if dropping the City in Turmoil provides a greater advantage to you or your opponent, and play it when necessary. City in Turmoil is one of the many tools to deal with Dragon Ball decks, but don't be afraid to use it in any advantageous scenario.

In summary, this is a veritable Swiss knife of a deck that can be very powerful when played to its full potential. You will find many of your games will involve a steady trading of hits, until you have breakout combat where you can deal lethal damage. The Anti-Anger and Anti-Dragon Ball tools are in the deck, but they are scarce. Utilize them efficiently to ensure a clean victory.

I hope you enjoy this deck as much as I do. I hope it can bring you success in your playing career. ✪

Regional Winner 2003

Main Personality:
1 Cell (Lv. 1) (Techno)
1 Cell, Stage Two (Lv. 2)
1 Cell, Perfect (Lv. 3)
1 Cell, the Destroyer (Lv. 4)
1 Cell, the Master (Lv. 5)

Mastery:
1 Namekian Style Mastery (TS)

Sensei:
1 North Kai Sensei [13]
3 Goku's Blinding Strike
3 Breakthrough Drill
3 Namekian Knee Strike
2 Namekian Offense SD
1 Hero's Drill SDO
1 Huh??? SDO

Defense:
3 Goku's Super Saiyan Blast
1 Nappa's Energy Aura
1 Goku's Energy Absorption
1 Super Saiyan Effect
1 Time is a Warrior's Tool
2 Pikkon's Leg Catch
3 Namekian Fist Dodge 3
3 Namekian Energy Deflection
3 Namekian Ducking Tech.
1 Yamcha's Skillful Defense
Namekian Energy Catch

Non-Combats:
1 Foreboding Evidence
1 Frieza is Ready
1 Where There's Life There's Hope

1 Champion Drill
1 Earth Dragon Ball 7
3 Krillin's Concentration
3 Piccolo and Heroes Gather
1 Fatherly Advice
1 Victorious Drill
1 Vegeta's Quickness Drill
1 Expectant Trunks

Attacks:
3 Namekian Dash
2 Gohan's Kick
2 Android 19s Energy Burst
3 Namekian Focused Blast
3 Vegeta's Jolting Slash
3 Namekian Quick Blast
3 Namekian's Strike
3 Namekian Eye Beam
1 Good Advice

Combats:
2 Aura Clash
1 Battle Pausing
2 Cell's Style
3 Trunks Energy Sphere
3 Namekian Energy Focus
1 Android 17 Smirks
3 Android 18's Stare Down
1 Stupid Tricks!
1 Cell's Presence
1 Cell's Threatening Position

Location Control:
1 Gohan's Nimbus Cloud
2 Cell's Instant Trans
2 City in Turmoil
2 Planet Vegeta

Killer Deck
Goku & Family

— By Matt Farrell

As the name suggests, this deck is built around Goku and his kin. Although it's a theme deck, it still has the capability to duke it out with the best of decks out there. It has a mix of powerful physical attacks and life draining energies, so you're bound to go down to the wire even with bad draws.

Throughout this game, Goku has always been one of the best personalities. Given this fact, I decided to build a deck around him. His level 1 and HT level 3 allow you to draw a card when entering Combat, and his level 2 lets you grab a card from the bottom of your discard pile. This means you'll always have an advantage over the competition, with one extra card.

With many level fours to choose from - and none with card advantage - I decided to throw in one that works well with Orange. His level 4 from the World Games saga allows you to get 5 Drills from either your discard pile or your Life Deck. Plus, with his high power stages, the beatdown will be just that much easier.

Orange has always been about energy, but when World Games arrived, the physical aspect finally came out. With +2 to all physical attacks, your +3s and +4s become +5 and +6, meaning your opponent will arrive at zero much quicker.

The South Kai Sensei will let you get Chi-Chi first turn. This will give you a physical block for every Combat, and make your opponent have to hit you one more time just to put a dent in your power stages. The other Allies are Gohan, Goten, and Videl, all members of Goku's family. In the Sensei deck are cards to help you deal with Dragon Ball decks, Huh??? being the premier Dragon Ball defense.

You also have physical attacks and blocks in this deck. Goku has one of the best physical attacks in the game. Goku's Physical Attack gives you two physicals, and each time one of them is successful, you get to draw the bottom card of your discard pile. Goku's Training is similar, but you can only use it once.

Gohan's Kick will help combat Dragon Ball decks and prevent your opponent from using cards like Time Is A Warriors Tool. Orange Searching Maneuver will let you get your Drills out much faster than just drawing them. Finally, one of my favorites, Orange Uppercut will let you get an Energy Combat card. Energy Combat is not an energy attack, so you can get a block or even Gohan's Nimbus Cloud (just in case your opponent puts a City in Turmoil on you). These blocks are standard blocks for a physical deck.

The energy attacks not only support the physical aspect of this deck, but also catch your opponent off-guard. Krillin's Solar Flare, if successful, will prevent your opponent from playing Physical Combat cards. If so, your physical attacks are likely to hit. Plus, your opponent can't play physical attacks that are Physical Combat cards.

Orange Scatter Shot is one of the best energy attacks in the game, so it needs to be played. Moreover, what Orange deck wouldn't be complete without Orange Stare Down? In addition, Non-Combat/Ally removal is a must in every deck. Orange Uniting Strike, not only has Endurance 3, but also does a whopping 8 life cards of damage if you have Gohan in play as an Ally. The energy blocks in this deck are great for defending your Life Deck from your opponent's nasty energy attacks.

As for Combat cards, not many

are needed in this deck. Time Is A Warriors Tool is the obvious choice. Confrontation can get rid of your opponent's one block, so you can unleash your physical attacks. Super Saiyan Effect will protect you against a physical onslaught and The Power of the Dragon can slow down those evil Dragon Ball decks.

Besides energy attacks, Orange's biggest strength is its board control. With the best Drills in the game, you will have your opponent wishing he'd put in more Drill removal. Each Drill in this deck serves a very important purpose. Android 20 Absorbing Drill and Orange Haulting Drill will help defend against your opponent's attacks, while Orange Joint Restraint Drill and Orange Aura Drill will make your attacks more powerful.

Vegeta's Quickness Drill adds another card to your hand, and Orange Destruction Drill ensures that your opponent won't crowd the table with Non-Combat cards. Expectant Trunks and Fatherly Advice let you get the one card you need to win the game.

Earth Dragon Ball 7 is a great comeback card. If you use it when your opponent enters, you can throw three Drills on top of your deck and you won't have to worry about drawing them during your opponent's turn, because it'll be your turn next. The locations in this deck are all searchable with Gohan's Nimbus Cloud and will help you Combat various deck-types you encounter.

Well, there you have it, the Goku Family Beatdown deck. Even the ladies of the family get in on the action. And who said theme decks couldn't be good, right? Remember when building a deck, don't be afraid to try something that hasn't been done before. There's no point in playing a game, if you can't have fun with it. Give this deck a try and good luck on your quest to become a champion. ✪

Goku's Family Beatdown (85 cards)

Main Personality: (4)
Goku, the Hero (CS)
Goku, the Saiyan (CS)
Goku, Earth's Hero HT (CS)
Goku, the King's Pupil (WG)

Mastery: (1)
Orange Style Mastery WG

Sensei: (1)
South Kai Sensei

Sensei Cards: (5)
2x Orange Rapid Attacks
1x Breakthrough Drill
1x Hero's Drill
1x Huh???

Physical Combat: (31)
4x Goku's Physical Attack
4x Goku's Training
3x Gohan's Kick
3x Orange Beatdown
3x Orange Searching Maneuver
3x Orange Uppercut
3x Orange Fist Catch
3x Tien's Block
3x Trunks Swiftly Moving
1x Nappa's Physical Resistance
1x Vegeta's Physical Stance

Energy Combat: (20)
3x Krillin's Solar Flare
3x Orange Scatter Shot
3x Orange Stare Down
3x Orange Uniting Strike
3x Orange Resistance
2x Goku's Super Saiyan Blast
1x Goku's Energy Absorption

1x Nappa's Energy Aura
1x Gohan's Nimbus Cloud

Combat: (9)
3x Confrontation
3x Trunks Energy Sphere
1x Super Saiyan Effect
1x The Power of the Dragon
1x Time Is A Warrior's Tool

Non-Combat: (11)
2x Android 20 Absorbing Drill
2x Orange Joint Restraint Drill
1x Orange Aura Drill
1x Orange Destruction Drill
1x Orange Haulting Drill
1x Vegeta's Quickness Drill
1x Don't You Just Hate That?
1x Expectant Trunks
1x Fatherly Advice

Dragon Balls: (1)
1x Earth Dragon 7

Allies: (4)
1x Chi-Chi Lv.1 (SS)
1x Gohan, the Great Saiyaman Lv.1 (WG)
1x Goten, the Playful Lv.1 (WG)
1x Videl, the Student Lv.1 (WG)

Locations: (3)
1x Hyperbolic Time Chamber
1x Protective Shelter
1x Winter Countryside

Cheap @$$ Deck

Maraikoh

Not Your Average Purple Dinosaur!!

Our Cheap @$$ Decks have no rare cards, so you build a decent deck, at a decent price!

Maraikoh is not your average purple dinosaur, and he'll prove it to anyone who dares to get in his way. His ability to physically overwhelm opponents will lock them down and leave them open for an all out assault.

Top Cards

The main card in this deck is none other than Maraikoh himself. His level 1 allows you to bomb rush your opponent in the early game, with two physical attacks dealing at least 5 power stages each. If you don't think that's enough, just wait until you get Cell's Arena into play and you'll be dealing more damage to your opponent than you can imagine.

It's why Cell's Arena is a key card in this deck. You don't need it to win, but if it gets into play, it can guarantee you the game. This Battleground will not only allow you to deal more damage with each attack, but it will also help you run your opponent out of power stages. He won't be able to perform any attacks against you.

If these effects aren't enough, Cell's arena will also allow you to lose enough power stages so your Allies can get a piece of the action. Recall that Allies can only take control of Combat if your Main Personality is at 0 or one power

— BY ISRAEL QUIROZ

stage above 0. Cell's Arena's drawback won't hurt you at all.

There is another card that can turn the tide of the game in a matter of seconds. It is none other than Alt. Dende Dragon Ball 2. This Dragon Ball's effect is aggressive and, when combined with Maraikoh's level one power, will be devastating.

As you can see, this deck loves modifiers that can make your Physical Attacks deal more damage, and that's exactly what the Dragon Ball does for you. It will also allow you to power up to full when you play it. You won't have to worry about being too low on power stages and locking yourself down with Cell's Arena.

How it Beats You

As you can see, this is a super aggressive deck that focuses on the early game. It doesn't really have anything for the late game, because with this deck there won't be a late game. If your opponent manages to stabilize, you'll have to attack him at every turn to keep him on the defensive.

If you're not an aggressive player (not willing to go into Combat without any blocks in hand and dealing as much damage as fast as possi-

Maraikoh

	1,390,000
	1,300,000
	1,210,000
	1,120,000
	1,030,000
	940,000
	850,000
	760,000
	670,000
	580,000
	0.000

Power: Physical attack doing 5 power stages of damage. If stopper, discard the top 2 cards of your Life Deck. If you declared a Taku-Weza, this power may be used twice per Combat.

Main Personality: (3)

Maraikoh HT Lv. 1
Maraikoh, the Strong
Maraikoh, the Mighty

Sensei: (1)

Grand Kai Sensei

Physical Combat: (48)

1x Nappa's Physical
    Resistance
1x Vegeta's Physical Stance
2x Black Face Smash
2x Black Reverse Kick
2x Black Chained Strike
2x Black Surprise maneuver
2x Black Quick Kick
3x Black Gravity Drop
3x Black Snap Kick
3x Black Personal Smack
3x Black Kick Lock
3x Black Light Jab
3x Black Reverse Strike
3x Black Face Slap
3x Gohan's kick
3x Black Palm Reversal
3x Black Defensive Stance
3x Black Wrist Block
3x Hidden Power Level

Energy Combat: (7)

1x Nappa's Energy Aura
3x Yamcha's Skillful Defense

3x Black Turning Kick

Combat: (8)

1x Time is a Warrior's Tool
1x Super Saiyan Effect
3x Trunk's Energy Sphere
3x Black Defensive Aura

Non-Combat: (10)

1x Alt. Dende Ball 2
1x Alt. Dende Ball 4
1x Black Weakness Drill
1x Black Anticipation drill
1x Black Shifting Drill
1x Black Double Attack Drill
1x Black Takedown Drill
3x Android 20 Absorbing
    Drill

**Battle Grounds/
Locations: (3)**

3x Cell's Arena

Allies: (5)

1x Krillin, the Friend
1x Goku, the Puppet
1x Gohan, the Furious
1x Goten, the Playful
1x Videl, the Student

Sensei Deck: (1)
HUH???

ble), this deck is not for you. When using this deck, you can not afford to play defensibly. If you try to set up before you start attacking your opponent, the odds are your opponent's deck will do a lot better late game than you will.

The purpose of this deck is to overrun your opponent early before he can set up, and hit him for as many Life Cards as you can. If you get lucky enough to hit his key cards in the early game, it'll take him a while to counter attack. I know what you're thinking, that it's crazy to hope to get lucky and hit the key cards right away, but keep in mind that this deck is aggressive enough to afford to such risks.

This deck will trade blow for blow, and it has enough power to race your opponent and run him out of cards before you're down for the count. Always keep in mind that this deck has to attack at every turn and entering Combat without any blocks in your hand is not such a bad thing. If you can force your opponent to lose all his power stages you'll be able to dominate him. Once you've reached that point, you'll be able to lock him down with Cell's Arena.

Your worst match-ups are Ally decks. They are slow by nature, which will only allow you to score a couple of decent hits before they can set up. If you hit your opponent before he can set up, you won't have to worry about him having too many Allies and you'll be able to dominate him. However, if he gets

a lucky draw and manages to stabilize right away, then all you can do is keep attacking like there's no tomorrow. If he gets too many Allies in play, there will be no tomorrow (for you).

Now you have learned all you can about the deck. Be as aggressive as you can be, and don't even consider skipping Combat if you have at least one attack in your hand. Maraikoh's power will give you two extra attacks and your opponent will have to be really lucky to stop three

Combat attacks. What may raise an eyebrow or two is the fact that even though this deck doesn't have a Mastery, it still declares a Tokui-Waza to get extra effects from the attacks in the deck.

If you can, try to get your hands on a Trunks Saga Black Style Mastery, because it can make the deck work better. If it's too hard to find that rare card, just have a blast beating your opponent with an all common and uncommon deck. =) ✪

Cheap @$$ Deck

Android 17's Allied Assault

It can be very difficult to build competitive decks without the best cards -- or even rares. Android 17 is simple to use, strong, and very inexpensive to build a deck around. He gives you a strong physical attack and ally removal all in one. This deck consists only of uncommons and commons, along with cards from the Cell Saga starter decks. This should give everyone a chance to go after Goku with the Androids.

TOP CARDS

On today's environment, personality powers are very important to the deck, which lead to Piccolo, The Trained's success, being that he can shut off his opponent's power every combat. So, why not strike back with Saiyan Inspection? This annoying little Non-Combat attaches itself to your opponent (so it'll work even if they lay down City In Turmoil afterwards). If they don't have Dragonballs, or you've already played your 3 and 5 and he's relying on playing is, you could have him locked down without a power for the remainder of the game!

The drill team in this deck is one of the orange variety. Orange Joint Restraint drill adds +4 power stages of damage to all of your physical attacks, most importantly your power. That's some major beef! If you start pulling off the double attacks like

– BY DAVID FASHBINDER

Majin Vegeta's Frantic Attack, you could be looking at a lot of damage. This card is a big menace to your opponent, and making them go on the defensive is great. This deck's appreance will catch them off guard very easily, passing you off as a weak threat due to your lack of rares.

Android 18's Pressure Routine from the Babidi Saga is a physical attack for +3 power stages of damage that forces your opponent to skip their +Attacker Attacks! phase every time they stop one of your attacks, for the remainder of combat, including the Routine itself! Comboing this with the powerful double attacks in your deck, like Frantic Attack and Red Shattering Leap, will cause your opponent to sit there in a daze if he plans on stopping any of your damage any time soon.

Your personality power should not be discounted. It is a physical that will hit from the D bracket as long as #17 is not at 0. It deals +3 power stages of damage, which could easily be enough to keep your opponent from attacking with a barrage of energies, and it will at least lower the amount of damage you're taking from physicals. The beauty of

having the ally support in this case is, if you're facing a nasty Piccolo, The Trained deck, your opponent will be forced to chose between your Main Personality and your allies!

WIN IT UP

Getting out your allies will only help you, especially against physical beatdown decks. Unexpected Company lets you grab both of them at the same time. Android 20 has a powerful energy attack that does +1 life card of damage for every android in play, including himself. So if he's out as Android 17's ally, that is 6 life cards of damage. This modifier is also affected by your opponent – so don't forget to deal more damage if he's playing androids himself. Cell's Arena should be used in conjunction with the allies to lock down your opponent by making every attack both of you play cost +1 power stage to perform. The attacks will also do +2 life cards of damage, so it raises the stakes. Just be careful that you do not drain yourself too much using the Arena.

Make sure you realize how many blocks you have in this deck. Many of the attacks also function as blocks, like Black Turning Kick and Blue Round Throw. There are also double blocks like Prepared Dodge, or its un-sphereable cousins, Yamcha's Skillful Defense and Black Defensive Stance.

Red Back Kick is a physical

A Beginner's Deck

Android 17 Lv. 1
Android 17 Lv. 2
Android 17 Lv. 3 HT

Allies: (4)
Android 20 Lv.1
Android 19 Lv. 1 (CS)
Guldo Lv. 1
Jeice Lv. 1

Locations: (3)
Cell's Arena x3

Physical Combat Cards: (28)
1x Vegeta's Physical Stance
1x Nappa's Physical Resistance
3x Red Power Lift
3x Blue Round Throw
3x Red Back Kick
3x Black Defensive Stance
3x Black Defensive Burst
3x Gohan's Kick
3x Red Shattering Leap
2x Android 18's Pressure Routine
3x Majin Vegeta's Frantic Attack

Energy Combat Cards: (18)
1x Nappa's Energy Aura
3x Yamcha's Skillful Defense
3x Blue Draining Blast
3x Black Turning Kick
3x Blue Arm Blast
3x Black Energy Web
2x Tien's Tri Beam

Combat Cards: (16)
1x Time is a Warrior's Tool
3x Blue Awakening
3x Blue Leaving
3x Mother's Touch
3x Prepared Dodge
3x Trunks Energy Sphere

Non-Combat Cards: (13)
1x Earth Dragonball 3
1x Earth Dragonball 5
1x Jeice Style Drill
1x Orange Destruction Drill
1x Orange Steady Drill
2x Orange Joint Restraint Drill
2x Saiyan Inspection
2x Unexpected Company
2x The Car

attack for +3 power stages of damage that not only lowers your opponent's anger level 1, it also stops ALL energy attacks for the remainder of combat – even focused ones!

Decks like Cell and his Cell Jrs and Ally En Masse with Z Warriors Gather are popular these days, and The Car is an efficient way to remove 2 of your opponent's allies from the game -- permanently. The Car is able to be searched out with Android 17's power so you don't have to

worry about drawing it when you need it the most.

So if you're new to DBZ or just feel like having an inexpensive second deck to practice against or take to fun local events, this deck should foot the bill. Be on the look out for some cards like Unexpected Allies and South Kai Sensei to increase your deck's chance of winning, but just remember that value is the most important thing in this case, and there is a lot of it here. ✪

Cheap @$$ Deck

Videl's the Rich Use the Poor's Physical Smackdown

— BY MATTHEW LOW

As we all know, Videl is the daughter of Hercule, which should make her the richest daughter on the face of earth. Hence, we would assume a deck featuring her would be full of cards that are extremely expensive. Not this time.

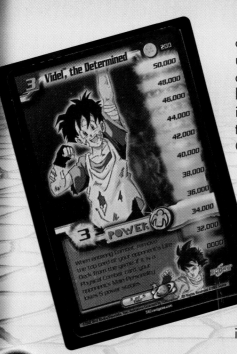

Videl has decided to twist the obvious and play with poor man's cards. Only commons and uncommons are used here, so you shouldn't have a tough time acquiring this collection. Pick up a Videl personality set, and you are ready to lay the Smackdown! You can smack Cell, Frieza, Buu, Android 17, or anyone, and show them that a girl can fight… with her fists of course.

The Power Cards

Of course, you can't have a deck without its power cards. These are the cards that give a deck its maximum potential, and this one is no different. As you might have noticed, it has no rares, ultra rares, promos, or uber rares. This deck may have a small pool of cards to work from, but it does take advantage of the sleeper commons and uncommons of Dragon Ball Z CCG.

Since we have no Mastery, we might as well not declare a Tokui-Waza and unlock Videl's plain wrong Level 2. If you do not declare a Tokui-Waza, it gives you TWO physicals for +4 stages. Of course, it's better than the broken Cell Level 1 HT (well, actually let's just plain wrong Cell Level 1 HT), except for power level and PUR (power up rating).

Videl's Level 1 HT is a focused physical attack for 3 stages that gains one anger no matter what, and more often than not will get a second if it hits. With that in mind, you should be able to get to level 2 in about three turns, maybe a little shorter if you use one of the many anger gaining cards in the deck. You can pretty much be assured that your level 2 is the level you'll be on for most of the game.

With a Level 2 power, the deck

builds and adds cards like Time Chamber Training and Orange Joint Restraint Drill to beef up the two guaranteed attacks. Two Time Chamber Trainings mean two physicals doing +6 power stages, and the Drill makes them +10. With the Drill in play, all your physical attacks do +4 power stages of damage. This will be welcomed nicely with cards that perform multiple physical attacks such as Black Triple Team and Red Shattering Leap.

After a well placed Gohan's Kick to make your opponent stay in combat and take a beating, lay the Smackdown with Videl's power twice and big modified physicals.

This deck continues with its modification of physical attacks to do more damage with the much overlooked Black Quick Kick and Black Palm Reversal. Quick Kick is a physical that can tack on 3 stages to every attack, noting that losing stages soon become life cards. With this card, energy attacks can be

denied very quickly.

Palm Reversal adds 3 discards to every attack, which is welcomed with open hands. The only stipulation is Quick Kick needs your opponent's board cleared of Non-Combats and Palm Reversal wants Drills gone. The quick and easy way to do this is Namek Dragon Ball 4.

However, since it is usually a one time shot, Red Lightning Slash can get rid of all Drills in one sweep, and Orange Temple Strike can sweep all non-combats at once, as long as you don't have any either. It even gets around the all-annoying Orange Focusing Drill. If any wandering Non-Combats are left, Red Energy Blast takes care of Drills while Gohan Meditates can get rid of Non-Combats.

I'm sure everyone knows that Piccolo the Trained can shut off your personality power. We also can agree it gets extremely annoying. Of course Videl wants to be just as annoying, so run Saiyan Inspection, which mimics Piccolo's power until your opponent either uses a Non-Combat Destruction card or put a Dragon Ball out.

While your opponent struggles to combat Saiyan Inspection, you pummel him with everything you have in your hand.

One of the most overlooked cards in the game is Master Roshi's Island. This Location punishes decks with a lot of named cards. Most deck carry quite a few of these cards. This deck runs a limited amount and thus shouldn't hurt from it.

With this Location, your opponent might have to think twice before attacking.

We also can't forget the annoying energy attack of Krillin's Solar Flare. I know you are probably wondering how Videl can perform energy attacks, let alone a Solar Flare. I'm still having a tough time imagining it. Videl and Solar Flare. The CCG says she can, so you might as well use the card.

It will throw a lot of people off guard as they will prepare for a physical onslaught. One of these will shut off the majority of your opponent's blocks, which will allow you to have a free-for-all with your physical attacks during a Combat.

Quick Walkthrough

When you start your game, you can either let your opponent know you are playing commons and uncommons only, or just keep your mouth shut. Either way, you'll mess with their mind. Playing with only commons and uncommons might make your opponent take it easy on you, whereas you won't.

On the other hand, most people who play without a Tokui-Waza play a card called Cosmic Backlash. It is a physical attack that allows you to win the game if you didn't declare one. Your opponent gets to draw five cards to stop your physical attack. If he can't, you win. Cosmic Backlash is a rare, so it is not in here.

However, if you don't say anything, your opponent will be scared to block some of your attacks in case a Backlash shows up. With Krillin's Solar Flare in here, your opponent may assume you have a Backlash as that card is its main setup.

You want to get to level 2 as soon as you can to take advantage of your level 2. A good strategy is to make the combat in which you jump from level 1 to 2 a big combat with one extra attack. Once at level 2, you want to stay there. Get Orange Joint Restraint Drill out as soon as you can, and attack with as many physical attacks as you can, modified with anything and everything, from Saiyan Blocking Technique to Time Chamber Training.

Against a Dragon Ball deck or a deck with only three levels, you may want to jump to level 3. There is a bit of anger in this deck, along with some good cards. At level 3, you can

remove a Dragon Ball from the game if you are lucky, and end up winning the game by default.

As for decks with three levels, you can win by Most Powerful Personality Victory.

This deck runs two sets of cards that both attack and block. Blue Round Throw is a big physical that can stop an energy, which can be a life saver if you need a block or it can be a beatdown weapon if you need one. Blue Arm Blast is there for a Cosmic Backlash. It can be played after Krillin's Solar Flare. Also, Yamcha's Skillful Defense is here for that reason as well.

Against Anger, you have Blue Defensive Effect and Namek Dragon Ball 3 to stall your opponent. With the other built-in anger reduction, you should be able to hold off Anger for a good amount of time.

Allies are easily discarded with Red Lightning Slash. Red Energy Blast picks up any slack as well. Red Energy Shield can work

two-fold and power your opponent's Main Personality to full if things go wrong.

With Namekian Energy being the greatest archetype, Red Back Kick and Straining Focusing Move fit nicely. They stop all energy attacks for combat, and seeing that you have few energy attacks, it will help you. After you do this a couple times, you might be able to beat up your opponent before you get hit once.

To Sum it Up

Check out this deck and see how it works. It is easy for a beginner to use, because it is combat oriented. Since you win using one method, the play is easy to grasp. There are cards in this deck that are ready to tech against nearly every main archetype; you have to learn to play it to perfection. Many cards included here are support cards to help you survive or to finish off your opponent. Good luck with using it, and attempt to develop your own combos to make it even better.

At first look, you can tell it is an easily made deck because it has no rares in it. If you want to make it better, you can do so by all

Main Personality – 3

Videl Level 1 HT WGS

Videl, the Protector Level 2 WGS

Videl, the Determined Level 3 WGS

Mastery – 0

Sensei – 0

Dragon Balls – 3

1 Namek Dragon Ball 2

1 Namek Dragon Ball 3

1 Namek Dragon Ball 4

Location – 3

3 Master Roshi's Island

Non-Combats - 6

1 Expectant Trunks

2 Time Chamber Training

3 Saiyan Inspection

Drills – 8

3 Orange Joint Restraint Drill

1 Orange Destruction Drill

1 Android 20's Absorbing Drill

1 Black Water Confusion Drill

2 Breakthrough Drill

Allies – 1

1 Krillin the Friend Level 1 CS

Physical Combat Attacks - 25

3 Red Shattering Leap

3 Red Back Kick

3 Gohan's Kick

3 Black Triple Team

3 Blue Round Throw

2 Straining Jump Kick Move

2 Red Lightning Slash

3 Black Quick Kick

3 Orange Temple Strike

Defense - 9

1 Vegeta's Physical Stance

1 Nappa's Physical Resistance

3 Saiyan Blocking Technique

2 Tien's Block

2 Black Palm Reversal

Energy Combat Attacks – 9

3 Krillin's Solar Flare

2 Red Energy Blast

3 Blue Arm Blast

1 Good Advice

Defense - 9

3 Straining Focusing Move

1 Nappa's Energy Aura

3 Yamcha's Skillful Defense

2 Red Energy Shield

Combat – 9

1 Time is a Warrior's Tool

1 Super Saiyan Effect

3 Trunks Energy Sphere

2 Blue Defensive Effect

2 Gohan Meditates

Total – 85

means. You should have fun working with it and modifying it to your liking.

The best part about this deck is after you win, you can smirk at your opponent and say he was just beaten by a girl who uses only commons and uncommons. Don't be mad at me when someone gets upset because they are beaten with this gem. The key is to have fun, and winning with a deck that is cheap (I know, bad pun) is fun.

If you ever want to share stories about how this deck has worked for you, or want tips on cards to make it better, feel free to email me at matthewlow@franceslow.com. I love to listen to your comments and will attempt to respond in a timely manner. After all, I'm here to help. ✪

Tuff Enough
Are You?

The Tuff Enuff (TE) format is by far the most played tournament outside of standard, and for good reasons. It takes the essence of the show (all out high action combat) and translates it directly into the card game. You can't win by the Most Powerful Main Personality Victory. You can't win by collecting all the Dragon Balls. Other than that, you abide by the normal rules of the CCG. One final new aspect that this format brings is the Overkill. If you perform an attack that deals 7 life cards more than your opponent has left, you've Overkilled them! For example, your opponent has 2 life cards left in his deck. You have the card "Villain's True Power" (Energy attack doing 10 life cards of damage) in your hand. You perform the attack successfully, and thusly overkill him, by dealing 7 or more cards of damage that your opponent does not have in his deck. This usually results in great prizes for you and your opponent is usually eliminated from the tournament.

— BY RICHIE WILLIAMS

So now that you know how you won't be winning, let's discuss how you will! The only ways to achieve victory in this format are Dragon's Victory (DV), Cosmic Backlash (CB), and of course Survival. DV and CB see more play in Tuff Enuff than they would in standard. This is for a few reasons, but mainly because they don't have to deal with Dragonball and Anger decks.

Krillin's Heat Seeking Blast

Energy Combat

POWER — Energy attack. This attack cannot be stopped or prevented. Remove from the game after use.

Dragon's Victory is a tricky archetype. It allows you to win by setting your anger to four and playing the card when your opponent is at either 3 or 4 anger. At first glance, this doesn't seem too difficult. Many players forget to take into account that many decks will be packing 3 Are You Tuff Enuff (Endurance 100. Raise all players anger 100) and perhaps even 3 Aura Clash (Raise all players anger 6). This can put quite a cramp in DV's style. There are various means to set up your opponent's anger for this style of deck. Before World Games Saga, DV was very popular in the TE format for Straining Double Strike Move (Physical doing 5 power stages of damage, raise your opponent's anger 1. Stays on table to be used once more). This was a Tuff Enuff exclusive card that easily raised your opponent's anger, making DV much more viable. Then with World Games Straining Cry Baby Move (Physical doing 5, raise opponent's anger 1) and Straining Diving Punch Move (Physical doing 5, raise opponent's anger 2) came along to further the ability of DV to set up the opponent's anger.

Even with a vast arsenal of new cards, DV still remains a rouge deck that requires style and skill to pull off. For this article, let's focus on a Red (TS) Master Roshi DV deck. Roshi's power is known for setting up the top 10 cards of your life deck, but his power also raises your anger 2 when entering combat if you declared a Red Touki Waza. That means in a short two combats time, your anger will be set at 4 without any

of the cards in your deck being dedicated to it. However, this can be messed with quickly. Since Roshi's ability to set up the top will allow you to draw what you need very quickly, keep the deck as close to the minimum as possible. If you enter first turn (Roshi will almost always start first at full due to the Double Power Rule) you should be able to set up your top to grab some of the straining cards to raise their anger and a DV. Remember, the key to this whole deck is going to be speed. You essentially must win before the opponent can even get a chance to start doing things. The

deck should contain 3 Straining Diving Punch Move, 3 Straining Double Strike Move, 3 Dragon's Victory (obviously), 1 Straining Rebirth Move (recycle your key cards in a late game situation), 3 Krillin's Concentration (pull the DV or other useful combat card), 3 Red Double Strike (when used with mastery, an instant 4 anger in a pinch), and then other staples like Trunks Energy Sphere, Confrontation, Battle Pausing, etc.

The next mode of victory, Cosmic Backlash, can be brutal-possibly even overkill you out of the tournament. One deadly card in this deck is Krillin's Solar Flare (energy attack, if successful your opponent may not use physical combat cards for remainder of combat). This energy attack can all but cripple your opponent's defenses against p h y s i c a l attacks, including your game w i n n i n g C o s m i c Backlash. R e d S h i e l d e d strike (physical disabling energy combat) and Piccolo's Fist Block (Combat card disabling your opponent's combat cards) also further ensure that the Backlash will be successful. Try other cards such as Stunned (auto win against certain characters), Caught Off Guard Drill, and Black Scout Maneuver to further manipulate your opponent's defenses. Be very wary of randomly playing the Backlash in hopes for a quick victory, as you will be giving your opponent 5 cards to beat you down with. In the Tuff Enuff format, these 5 cards will almost certainly be all out beef in order to finish you off with.

The final mode of vic-

tory, Survival, gives a player much more options than the previous two archetypes. Backlash and DV require specific cards to acquire victory, while Survival can beat the opponent down in a variety of ways. Are you a fan of the Black Style with its versatile array of powerful physical and energy attacks, not to mention cards that can both attack and block? Do you enjoy the fist full of physical attacks the Saiyan style will give you? Do you prefer a calm, controlling beat down over a course of time from the Blue Style? As you can see, a player has many more choices to decide how they will win using the Survival mode of victory. Decks to watch out for involve Saiyan Majin Vegeta, Lord Slug Regeneration, and Krillin Blue.

One of the most popular TE decks that we will investigate in depth involves Krillin. His World Games level 3 makes Krillin's H e a t

ly fast in both winning and losing. If you did not declare a Touki Waza, this single card can end the game. However, the opponent does get to draw 5 cards when you play it. Cosmic Backlash decks must keep the minimum deck size, 50, in order to draw the key cards as quickly as possible. Again, let's focus on Master Roshi for this archetype (I hate to use him in two examples, please don't think he's the best Main Personality in the card game, or even Tuff Enuff for that matter). Backlash is all about immobilizing the cards the opponent is allowed to use and then ending the game. However, the speed of the deck is a double edged sword. Such a small deck also means your opponent only need's to deal a small amount of damage to end the game, and

Seeking Blast (which he can play four of), or any energy for that matter, a game ending overkill hit. Combine that with the fact that 3 Aura Clash and 3 Are You Tuff Enuff with 3 Anger Management make leveling up on the way quite brutal as well. A simple combo such as Anger Management and Aura Clash can make your level two deal 28 life cards of damage on its own. A Tien's Tri Beam can be used three times, doing 12 life cards each hit. This is all without taking into account that his level three can be boosting these attacks by as many as 30 power stages! Since there will be a huge amount of Krillin named cards to feed his level three, the Capsule Corp Power Pack II provides a nice level one for this deck. The Blue Style Mastery (CS) gives a defense per turn to bide your time until you unleash lethal damage unto your opponent. Not to mention you gain cards like Blue Terror and

Blue Krillin Tuff Enuff

1 Krillin (Level 1)(CCPP)
1 Krillin (Lv. 2) (Techno)
1 Krillin, the Great (Level 3)
1 South Kai Sensei [5]
1 Blue Style Mastery (CS)
4 Krillin's Solar Flare
4 Krillin's Search
4 Krillin's Heat Seeking ...
1 Earth Dragon Ball 7
4 Krillin's Energy Attack
4 Krillin's Physical Defense
3 Krillin's Concentration
4 Krillin Unleashed
2 Krillin Ask For Help
4 Krillin's Power Block
1 Bubbles Drill
1 Battle Pausing
3 Confrontation
3 Anger Management
3 Arqua's Arena
1 Victorious Drill
1 Expectant Trunks
1 Fatherly Advice
2 Piccolo and Heroes Gather
3 Tien's Tri-Beam
1 Blue Terror
2 Blue Energy Trans.
3 Are You Tuff Enuff???
2 Gohan Meditates
1 Super Saiyan Effect
3 Trunks Energy Sphere
1 Vegeta's Physical Stance
1 Nappa's Physical Resistance
1 Nappa's Energy Aura
1 Time's a Warrior's Tool
1 Gohan, Great Saiya. (Lv. 1)
1 Piccolo, the Avenger (Lv. 1)
1 Maraikoh (Lv. 1)
1 Nail The Namekian (Lv. 1)
2 Blue Leaving
2 He's Safe
3 Aura Clash

Blue Leaving to further set up your various combos. There is a nice side of ally in the deck to deal with early physical onslaughts, not to mention to provide even more energy attacks once you get Krillin to low enough stages. As many named cards as possible are included in the deck to make his level three as effective as possible. In fact, this is one of the few decks where taking life cards of damage can actually help you to win! I think everyone has the general idea of how to work this deck now, so without further ado... ✪

Tuff Enough
Cell's Return

Majin Buu has arrived and thinks he's big and bad, but Cell will soon teach him he's nothing but a pink blob. It's time for a blast from the past and there's no stopping Cell's rampage.

— BY ISRAEL QUIROZ

Top Cards

The release of the Majin Buu Saga has brought new moves to an old fighter. Cell, the master of Physical attacks, now has Majin Buu's Fury to stop his opponents dead in their tracks and keep them from doing anything but attack. Majin Buu's Fury is one of the best cards in this deck to lock down any type of combo deck. Once you play it, your opponent has no choice but to attack during his attacker attacks phase or pass. It's that simple.

The Namekian Style didn't get anything in the Babidi Saga. There was only one Namekian card in the set, and it was not a very playable drill. The player base began to believe the Namekian style had been forgotten. However in the Buu Saga, it's a different story. Namekian Shuto

and Namekian Shield Destruction give the Namekian Style removal (being able to destroy Allies and Non-Combat cards). Both cards have decent Endurance as well.

This deck has removal and a new way to stop combo decks but it still needs something else. How about Master Roshi's Sensei? Yup, this Sensei doesn't only make all attacks you perform deal more damage, but it also prevents one Life Card from every attack your opponent performs. Preventing one Life card might not seem like much, but you'll be surprised at the difference it makes in the game.

How it Beats You

It's very simple. Cell didn't come back to play games, he physically destroys any deck your opponent can throw at him. If you don't believe me, look at how many Physical attacks this deck is packing and how it is so Combat-oriented. This deck will attack your opponent every single turn and lock any deck down early in the game.

Cell's power, which you can use two times per Combat every Combat, combined with the card

drawing ability of the Namekian Style Mastery, will allow you to rush your opponent early in the game. After that point, all you need to do is to keep attacking and prevent your opponent from stabilizing.

You want to make sure you play Gohan's Kick or Majin Buu's Fury as your first card in Combat. These two cards will disrupt your opponent and keep him from ending Combat or trying to pull nasty tricks that may allow him a come back.

You may think this deck can play itself, and that it's impossible to make a mistake because all do is play attack after attack, but don't let this ease of play fool you. The worst thing you can do while playing this deck is get overconfident. You can't stop paying attention to your opponent and what he's trying to do.

The deck is a lot of fun to play and sometimes you can make small mistakes without realizing it. You're having a blast flinging Physical after Physical attack at your opponent and don't keep your mind in the game.

This deck's biggest weakness is that it doesn't grow during the game, and all you have is Physical attacks with a decent amount of disruption. Although, that may seem to be all you need at times, if you ever let your opponent stabilize he'll give you a run for your money. Try to attack every turn if possible and don't ever skip more than two Combats or it can cost you the game.

This deck's biggest threat is Ally decks. However, once you Sensei, you have more ways to deal with those pesky Allies. As

-MP Cards- 5

Cell, Stage One (HT)
Cell, Stage Two
Cell, Perfect
Cell, the Destroyer
Cell, the Master

-Mastery- 1

Namekian Style Mastery (TS)

-Sensei- 1

Master Roshi Sensei

-Combat Cards- 17

X3 Trunks Energy Sphere
X3 Are You Tuff Enuff???
X3 Android 18s Stare Down
X3 Namekian's Strike
X2 Cell's Presence
X1 Battle Pausing
X1 Time is a Warriors Tool
X1 Super Saiyan Effect

-Physical Combat- 51

X4 Cell's Backslap
X3 Namekian Elbow Smash
X3 Namekian Shuto
X3 Namekian Shield
   Destruction
X3 Namekian Face Smack
X3 Namekian Dash Attack
X3 Namekian Side Kick

X3 Namekian Fist Smash
X3 Namekian Light Jab
X3 Majin Buu's Fury
X3 Gohan's Kick
X3 Goku's Training
X3 Goku's Physical Attack
X3 Namekian Ducking
   Technique
X3 Namekian Fist Dodge
X3 Namekian Charging
   Stance
X1 Vegeta's Physical Stance
X1 Nappa's Physical
   Resistance

-Energy Combat- 10

X3 Krillin's Solar Flare
X3 Yamcha's Skilful Defense
X2 Goku's Super Saiyan
   Blast
X1 Nappa's Energy Aura
X1 Frieza's Force Bubble

-Non-Combat- 3

X2 Android 20 Absorbing
   Drill
X1 Frieza is Ready

-Sensei Deck- 9

X3 Cookies!!!
X3 Namekian Knee Strike
X2 Horrified
X1 Hero's Drill

for your Sensei Deck, make sure you always add Hero's Drill and you'll be fine.

You should get out there and have a blast beating down your opponent. This deck's super fast and you shouldn't be surprised if half of your opponent's deck is gone after the first turn. Who dares say an old villain can't come back and crush every new and old hero? ✪

Tuff Enough

Everkrillin'

– BY DAVE FASHBINDER 'DBM'

This is a modified version of the deck that I won the Shonen Jump Launch Event with, back in 2002. It packs a pretty mean punch, disguised in a little bald package.

Krillin, the Great 135

775,000
725,000
675,000
625,000
575,000
525,000
475,000
425,000
375,000
325,000
275,000
225,000
0000

3

4 POWER

Constant Combat Power: All energy attacks you perform do +1 power stages of damage for every Named card in your discard pile. At the beginning of your turn, remove 2 Named cards in your discard pile from the game.

3 of 3
Krillin

There are three major 'combos' in this deck. The first one is the crux of the design. Anger Management + Are you Tuff Enuff??? / Aura Clash. Combining the 2 cards allows all of your attacks for the remainder of combat to do an upwards of 10 additional life cards. If you can manage to stack multiple Anger Management, all your attacks will do even more. Jumping from level 1 to level 2 with this maneuver provides you with 2 attacks doing a lot of damage, and the first one drawing 1 card for each Anger Management played. This combo works with the 2 'multiple-use' energy attacks in the deck : Krillin's Energy Attack and Tien's Tri-Beam. Using this method you can easily deal over 100 life cards of damage.

The second combo is Krillin's level 3 power + named cards. This deck is freestyle, so the majority of cards are named. Get to the level 3, with or without the Anger Management combo, and you'll be dealing major damage, especially if you search out Krillin's Heat Seeking Blast with the great new Freestyle Mastery.

The third combo is South Kai Sensei to grab Tien, The Swift in order to draw cards with your Tien's Jolting Auras. Don't be afraid to take damage in this deck, or to sandbag on your ally, because once you get to that

Krillin (CCPP2)
Krillin, The Hero (HT)
Krillin, The Great (WGS)
Freestyle Mastery (MBS)
South Kai Sensei (WGS)

Allies:
Tien, The Swift (CS)

Dragonballs:
Earth Dragon Ball 7 (SS)

Locations/Battlegrounds:
Arqua's Arena x3 (WGS)

Non-Combat:
Vegeta's Quickness Drill x1 (SS)
Android 20 Absorbing Drill x2 (TS)
Bubbles Drill x1 (Promo)
Fatherly Advice x1 (Promo)
Expectant Trunks x1 (TS)
Piccolo and Heroes Gather x3 (TS)
Krillin's Concentration x4 (FS)
Victorious Drill x1 (Promo)

Energy Combat:
Krillin Unleashed x4 (CS)
Krillin's Energy Attack x4 (SS)
Krillin's Heat Seeking Blast x4 (TS)

Krillin's Solar Flare x4 (CS)
Tien's Tri-Beam x3 (CS)
Tien's Jolting Aura x3 (FS)
Nappa's Energy Aura x1 (SS)

Physical Combat:
Krillin's Face Slap x2 (Promo)
Krillin's Power Block x4 (FS)
Vegeta's Physical Stance x1 (SS)
Nappa's Physical Resistance x1 (SS)

Combat:
Are You Tuff Enuff??? x3 (Promo)
Anger Management x3 (Promo)
Gohan Meditates x3 (CGS)
He's Safe x2 (Promo)
Time Is A Warrior's Tool x1 (FS)
Trunks Energy Sphere x3 (TS)
Super Saiyan Effect x1 (TS)
Confrontation x3 (Promo)
Battle Pausing x1 (SS)
Aura Clash x2 (CGS)
Krillin's Search x4 (Promo)
Krillin's Physical Defense x4 (SS)

level 3, all your attacks that hit will be doing 20-40 life easily.

Most situations in Tuff Enuff will dictate being hit with a lot of attacks. The card Krillin's Power Block is very versatile in Tuff Enuff. Physical Beatdown is extremely popular, with Cell HT and Majin Vegeta running around. This card will not be removed from the game if you're sticking it out on Level 1. The Level 1 may be where you need to get a lot of work done, especially if you get smacked with Winter Countryside until you can get the empowering Arqua's Arena into play. The more versatile cards on level 1 are Krillin's Search and his Heat Seeking Blast, amazing cards that will be able to stick around and if not used again, will at least boost your level 3's power.

The biggest weakness this deck has is its absolute lack of blocks. This does give a drastic disadvantage to Cosmic Backlash, so metagame as needed. Change your deck slightly if CB is played big time in your area. Do not be alarmed otherwise, the damage you take will be great to take advantage of if you conserve your leveling resources, Are You Tuff Enuff??? and Aura Clash. ✪

Sealed Deck Tournament Format

How to Play

— BY ISRAEL QUIROZ

A sealed deck tournament is a special tournament where you don't play with your own deck. You are given a starter deck and three booster packs and have to build a deck out of whatever cards you get. The outstanding feature of this format is it generally allows you to declare a Rainbow Tokui-Waza.

Declaring a Rainbow Tokui-Waza means you get a +1 PUR (Power Up Rating) bonus for your main personality and get all the Tokui-Waza effects on your cards, while being able to play cards from different styles in your deck. This special Tokui-Waza allows every card to be used to its full potential and the extra +1 PUR helps you play energy attacks.

If that isn't enough, when you're allowed to declare a Rainbow Tokui-Waza, you can use any Mastery that you might get in your starter deck or in your three booster packs. Sounds like a blast doesn't it? Being able to declare a Rainbow Tokui-Waza is one of the main reasons why players like the format. If you've never played in one ask your local retailer to organize the event and prepare for the unexpected.

There currently aren't a lot of Sealed Deck events on the circuit, other than Pre-releases, but it's still important to be prepared because you never know when it might become a major competitive format. In a Sealed Deck event, your deck building skills and knowledge of the format are what determine how well you do, so let's review what we have learned.

Know the Environment

There are two major elements about this format that often determine how well you compete – luck and skill. The first factor is luck and there isn't much you can do about it, except pray that you get good cards. Skill is the one feature you can control and what will give you an edge over the other players, or give your opponent the game. What the outcome will be depends on how much effort you're willing to put into this format.

The first thing you want to do is be prepared and have a game plan. What many players don't know is that a Sealed Deck Tournament begins long before the day of the event. You should find out what sets will be used in the Sealed Deck event and take the time to look over what each of these sets have to offer. Review the commons and uncommons of each of the sets that will be used and make notes on whether those sets have more Energy Attacks, Physical Attacks, Energy Blocks or Physical Blocks.

Gaining this knowledge will help you decide what type of deck you'll want to build and will help you figure out what most players will be using.

If you have the time you might also want to review the rares of each set, but since you won't be seeing many of them I suggest you spend your time studying the cards that can make a difference, like Anger. Anger is one of the most overlooked strategies in a sealed environment because players just aren't used to seeing a lot of Anger decks. The assumption is that if Anger decks don't work in Constructed, then they clearly won't work in a Sealed Deck environment.

This assumption is wrong, because if there's enough Anger in the sets being used it can be the easiest victory to achieve. After all, your deck only needs to gain a total of 10 Anger to win the game. Granted, it will only happen if your opponent doesn't have a level 4 as a Main Personality. However, I wouldn't worry because it's very unlikely a player will get a level 4 that matches his Main Personality in a Sealed Deck event.

Even if you feel there isn't enough Anger in the environment to win, it can still make a difference. Look over all the Main Personalities that pop up and see if any of them can gain you Anger, or if their level two's are worth trying to reach. There are times when you want to stay on your level one with certain personalities, and that's why it's better to consider these options ahead of time instead of trying to figure out your game plan when you receive your cards during the tournament.

Building your Deck

I can't stress how important it is

through the various scenarios beforehand to be prepared when the time comes.

Choosing your Attacks

Your attacks are the way to victory and without them you won't be able to pressure your opponent. If you don't have enough, you'll be a sitting duck; and, if you have too many, you'll leave yourself open for a beatdown. Use your knowledge of the environment to figure out how many attacks you want in your deck and what type of attacks you want to use.

It is during this phase of deck building that you'll meet your biggest dilemma: do you want to use Physical Attacks, Energy Attacks or both? I would approach it in the same manner. Take all of your cards that perform attacks and divide them into three piles. The first pile contains attacks that are a "must". These have great effects or deal tremendous amounts of damage.

The second stack would contain all Energy Attacks, and the third one all Physical attacks that didn't make the first pile.

With this method, you can identify the number of attacks you must use, and two piles to help determine what type of attacks to focus on. The decision regarding the type of attacks to focus on is a difficult one. I struggle with it, but I believe one type is better than the other. To explain, I'll

to build a good deck, and why you can't afford to make any mistakes in the process. Your first move should be to separate your cards into four different piles: Blocks, Energy Attacks, Physical Attacks and Miscellaneous.

Choosing your Blocks

I personally believe that having enough blocks in your deck is one of the most, if not the most important factor. A deck with a low number of blocks simply doesn't have a chance, because the main victory condition in this format is survival. Keep this in mind when you're deciding how many blocks you're going to use.

Always remember that even if you receive all the best cards, it won't do any good if they're hit as Life Cards of damage.

Once you have your blocks set aside, you have to decide what type you want to use. In regular, you might think using half-and-half is the best way to go. However, a simple decision like this one can cost you the tournament. This is a time when being prepared will pay off.

Don't forget that you have already looked over the sets being used and know what type of attacks most players will be using. You also need to keep other factors in mind. Even if there are more Physical attacks in the environment, you might have to use more Energy Blocks if most personality's level one powers can perform Energy attacks. Again, you have to run walk you through my self-learned process so you can understand my rationale.

Energy Attacks Vs Physical Attacks

Both types of attacks have their advantages and disadvantages. What I consider the best thing about Physical Attacks is that you don't have to pay for most of them. You can play a Physical Attack when your Main Personality is at 0 and you have no power stages left. The downside is that you have to work your opponent down before you can deal any Life Cards.

Physical Attacks can help you keep your opponent at low power stages, but if he's also focusing on Physical Attacks, it won't impact his play.

Energy attacks, on the other hand, go straight to your opponent's Life Deck. It doesn't matter whether or not they have a high PUR, their deck can gain a lot of power stages and you don't help them if they happen to pull any Allies.

The major drawback of Energy attacks is the fact that most require you to pay power stages, and if your opponent hits you with Physical after Physical Attack you won't be able to do anything to him. Even with this disadvantage, I still like Energy Attacks more than Physical attacks. It may seem crazy to focus on Energy over Physical

in a limited environment, but I do have my reasons.

The first consideration is if you get a Hero Starter deck, you will always have one Ally that can help because there's always a Hero Ally in every starter deck for the battle simulator. If you have an Ally, and you play your cards right, you'll always be able to pay for Energy attacks because you can redirect all Physical damage to your Ally.

The next factor to consider is if you have a high PUR, you'll be able to play at least two Energy Attacks when you declare Combat. You can start with the first one and, if you have at least one Physical Block, you'll be able to protect your power stages. If so, it will allow you a

second Energy Attack at your opponent.

Physical attacks are more reliable and, if you can lock down your opponent, your deck will work well until they get an Ally into play. Energy attacks may be risky but deal damage where it counts. Don't let my personal preference influence your deck building. I am not encouraging you to make a heavy Energy Attack deck in your next Sealed Event. After all, it's only my personal preference and all players must have their own unique play styles.

Now that you've decided how many blocks and what type of attacks you'll want to use, your deck is practically ready to go. The last thing you want to do is

Sealed Decks - How To Play

look over your other cards and see if any of them can help you. Other than using every Ally you can play (whether you're leaning toward Physical or Energy attacks), there's no major rules to follow or keep in mind. Most Sealed Decks I've seen run a lot of Attacks, Blocks and whatever Allies they can use, because most Non-Combat cards won't make a difference in the game. However, there are some exceptions, so don't shut your door on Non-Combats before you've looked over them.

As I've described, the only other factor to bear in mind in a Sealed Deck Event is that luck plays a powerful role. You shouldn't feel bad if you

build the best deck but lose every game against better decks. I've seen great players eliminated in the first two rounds of Sealed Deck Events, and I've also seen new kids go all the way to the finals because of the good cards they got in their decks. At the end of the day, having fun is all that matters, but if you're like me and enjoy building decks with a limited card pool, you'll have a blast in a Sealed Event. =) ⬤

Premiere Events

— BY ISRAEL QUIROZ

Have you ever wondered about a Premiere Event? What it is and what makes it better than your local tournament? Maybe you've wondered how often these events happen and where they are located. If you have ever considered any of these questions, I'm here to help you understand them.

A premiere event can be a lot of things. It can be anything from a Regional Tournament or World Championship to what's sometimes called a Super Sized event. These so-called "Premiere Events" are tournaments planned and run by Score Entertainment.

Regional tournaments are the most common events. They are large gatherings with special support and are usually organized and run by a Score Entertainment representative. According to many players, any tournament where a Score Entertainment representative is found is a Premiere Event. Score Entertainment employees usually bring enough extra support to make the tournament an outstanding event.

A Super Sized event is a normal tournament where a Score Entertainment Representative will be present to help run it and provide extra support.

I guess you could say as a rule of thumb if there is a Score Entertainment representative present you've got a Premiere Event. Prizes awarded at these events for the winner and the participant are usually better than a local tournament as well.

How Can I find Premiere Events?

Regardless of whether the event is a major tournament or just a Super Sized outing, there will always be information about it on Score Entertainment's official website. Make sure you check dbzcardgame.com regularly to stay informed about where and when Premiere Events will happen.

Regional tournaments usually take place at conventions while Super Sized events are normally found in stores all over the country. You never know where the next Super Sized event will happen because they don't occur very often and it doesn't appear Score Entertainment plans them ahead of time like regional events.

Super Sized Events often seem to be spur of the moment activities that are put together two weeks before they happen. They seem to pop out of nowhere and the players don't get much time to prepare for them. Given this fact, it pays to check the official website regularly and even check a few message boards when you can, to get as much notice about such events as possible.

Why aren't there any Premiere Events near me?

Score Entertainment tries to sponsor major events all over the country but it's not possible to organize one in every city because there are many factors involved. Regional and major tournaments occur at certain comic book conventions that are generally hosted at the same

place every year. As I've described, the Super Sized events have no set schedule and occur randomly.

If you would like Score Entertainment to run a Super Sized event near you or at your local store, there are things you can do to make it happen. Score Entertainment will only consider Super Sized events at stores that are proactive and care about their players, so the best thing a local store owner can do is to give Score Entertainment a send them an e-mail. Score Entertainment tries to run its Super Sized events at different locations, but if the store owners aren't

interested or don't publicize the event, it is canceled and forgotten.

If your local store owner calls Score Entertainment to inquire about hosting a Super Sized event, there's no guarantee that one will happen immediately, but you can be sure that the next time Score Entertainment is looking for a location in the area they will consider that store.

I know that Score Entertainment is always looking for new locations and for better ways to organize more Premiere Events every year. You can be certain that one will be held in your area at some point. How soon it happens is up to your local store owner.

What are you waiting for? Tell your store owner to e-mail Score Entertainment and don't be surprised when representatives show up to scout for one of these super cool, Super Sized events. =) ✪

Dragon Ball Z CCG

Top Ten Lists

– BY ISRAEL QUIROZ

Saiyan Saga

1. Vegeta's Quickness Drill

After looking over the Saiyan Saga time after time, it's not hard to see why this is the best card in the set. This drill is a powerful card that allows you to draw one extra card every time you enter Combat, whether you're the attacker or the defender. Most cards that allow you to draw cards every turn usually hurt you in the long run, because you end up running out of cards. With this card you draw cards from your discard pile, so you'll never have to worry about running out of cards.

2. Earth Dragon Ball 7

This card is the best Dragon Ball out of the Saiyan Saga. It doesn't only end Combat to buy you more time, but it also allows you to set up your next turn. When you play this card you can choose any three cards from your discard pile and place them at the top of your Life Deck in any order. This is the best combo set up ever. You not only get to end Combat, but you get to set up your hand for your next turn.

3. Battle Pausing

This Combat card has been a powerhouse ever since it was released. Score slowly started to weaken this card by changing its power and restricting it to one per deck. After that, it's power was changed to draw the top two cards from your discard pile, remove from the game after use, limit one per deck and your opponent's Main Personality gained five power stages. Still, despite these modifications, the card is still playable and it screams to be used in combo decks.

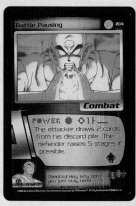

4. Teaching the Unteachable Force Observation

Being able to end Combat is usually good when you're trying to set up and finish off you opponent. However, being able to keep your opponent from attacking you is much better. There are times when you can't afford to have your opponent attack you, because you may run out of cards or your combo is almost ready. In that instance, this card comes into play as it gives you the ability to keep your opponent from attacking you. You'll have all the time you need to make a comeback or to set up a killer combo to finish him off.

5. Saiyan Truce Card

There may be a lot of cards that can end Combat and protect you from your opponent, but this card stills stands out among the rest. The ability to end Combat alone would make it worthwhile. By getting to keep all the cards in your hand while your opponent still has to discard his cards, it simply screams to be abused. This card was and is still being used in many decks. Before this card was restricted to one per deck, Beatdown Decks were able to crush their opponents. With this card they were able to keep up to twenty cards in their hand.

6. Vegeta's Physical Stance

It's not often that one can find a card that will shut down your opponent in a heartbeat. If your opponent is trying to take you out with big, fat physical attacks, this card is all you need to stop him. No matter how strong your opponent is, Vegeta's Physical Stance stops all of his Physical attacks for one turn. When you're facing a Physical Beatdown Deck, you'll be glad you have this card because it'll help you if you're in a tight spot. It can turn the tide of the game, since your opponent won't be able to harm you while you can still hit him with your Physical attacks.

7. Orange Focusing Drill

One of the hardest things to deal with in this game is a good Non-Combat set up. This drill might not do much alone, but once you start getting your other drills in play, it's all you need to keep them safe. This drill protects your other drills from being discarded, and it forces your opponent to destroy it first before he can do anything to your other drills. This is the card set up players have been dreaming about because it will frustrate your opponent in more ways than you can imagine.

8. Goku's Capturing Drill

This drill is the reason Dragon Ball Decks have been around so long. With this drill in play, your opponent will never be able to steal your Dragon Balls and there won't be anything he can do to stop you. It really is that simple. Get this drill in play and you can start to play your Dragon Balls without worrying about them being captured by your opponent. This drill works even if he deals you five or more Life cards of Damage. When it comes to Dragon Ball Deck cards, it just doesn't get any better than Goku's Capturing Drill.

9. Ally Wins

If you like to hit your opponent with cards he won't be able to stop, you'll love this card. This Combat card forces your opponent to discard one life card for each ally you have in play. It might not do a lot of damage in the early game, but later on it can be a game finisher. The one thing that makes this card great is the fact that only one card in the entire game can stop it. If your opponent doesn't have it when you play this card, it will be fifteen life cards he won't be able to stop.

10. Red Back Kick

This card is greatly underestimated and, for some odd reason, not many players use it. It is a Physical attack dealing +3 power stages of damage that stop all energy attacks for the remainder of Combat and lower your opponent's anger one anger level. The card is decent and is a must in every Red Deck, because that style doesn't have a lot of cards that can stop Energy attacks. Red Back Kick is one of those cards that can protect you while beating down your opponent. It would be silly not to use it.

Frieza Saga

1. This Too Shall Pass

Ladies and gentlemen, set your eyes on the best card in the game. It is not best because of what it can do, but because of what it can keep your opponent from doing. This card simply cancels any card that your opponent uses against you, and he will lose all the effects from that card. It's no surprise that it is not legal in tournaments (but it's still the best card in the game.)

2. Time is a Warrior's Tool

Talk about cards that just say no to your opponent's attacks, Time is a Warrior's Tool is a master. This card stops all of your opponent's Energy and Physical attacks without even removing itself from the game. Its only downside is that it's limited to one per deck. However, when you keep in mind how strong it is, that is hardly a drawback.

3. Orange Destruction Drill

The Saiyan Saga was all about playing Dragon Ball Decks and using decks with a lot of Non-combat cards. This card changed the environment because of its ability to destroy any Non-Combat card in play at the beginning of every turn. What may take your opponent several turns to set up is destroyed by this card in a matter of seconds. As long as there are playable Non-Combat cards in the game, there will always be room in a deck for this card.

4. Frieza Smiles

The Frieza Saga doesn't have a lot of strong attacks, but it does have what you need to stop them. This card is one of many that can completely shut down your opponent and keep him from harming you during Combat. It is also the kill card in a lot of Dragon Ball Decks. With this card, you can stop all of your opponent's attacks while you use Non-Combat cards to get your Dragon Balls into play.

5. Guldo Lv. 1

This card is the best personality the Frieza Saga brought to the table. The green guy's Physical attack might not deal a lot of damage, but it allows you to draw two more cards from the bottom of your discard pile every time you use it. Guldo has made what would be long games last less than ten minutes. His power allows you to overwhelm your opponent by drawing an insane amount of cards per turn.

6. Mommy's Coming Dear

This card's image is a reminder of how scary women can be. Just kidding. Although this card may not seem like much because it stops all of the damage from your attacks, it can save you if you're trying to stay alive or have no attacks in your hand. Combo it off with Earth Dragon Ball Seven and you won't take any damage from your opponent's attacks.

7. Jeice's Style Drill

This drill is one of those cards that seem ok when they are released, but get better as time goes on. It used to be just another drill that can stop attacks from your opponent, but now it's better than all the new defense shields. Since it's not a defense shield, it can stop focused attacks. However, you have to make sure it's the first Energy attack played or it won't work.

8. Vegeta's Jolting Slash

If you're using a villain, this card is a definite must. It's a nice Energy attack that stops all Physical attacks against villains, and it also lowers your opponent's anger two anger levels. Once you add up all of the benefits, you have a card that can do three really nice things and it only costs two power stages. Use Vegeta as your Main Personality, plus you can have up to four of these babies in your deck.

9. Straining Focusing Move

We've seen a lot of cards that can stop Physical attacks, but there aren't a lot of cards that can do the same for Energy attacks. This Straining Move is one of the few cards that can stop Energy attacks. If you think about how Energy attacks usually deal life cards while Physical attacks deal power stages, you realize how much better a card is that stops Energy attacks compared to a card that stops Physical attacks.

10. Yamcha's Skillful Defense

Last but not least, we have a card that's been seen in a lot of decks since it was released. We can think of cards that can stop either a Physical attack or an Energy attack, but they're all Combat cards. It might not seem like much, but Combat cards can be canceled by Trunks Energy Sphere, even when they're blocks. Cards like this one can't be canceled by anything.

Trunks Saga

1. Chiaotzu's Psychic Halt

This card is wrong in many ways. When you play it, your opponent can't do a single thing at all. They can't use Non-Combat cards, allies, play attacks or anything. This card alone used to determine games because of it's amazing power. You won't be seeing it in tournaments anymore, but it's still the best card in the Trunks Saga.

2. Trunks Energy Sphere

Say hello to one of the few "counter spells" that Score hasn't banned, and it doesn't look like it will be banned in the near future. This card is what gamers call "counter spells" because it can stop your opponent from doing anything he may be trying to achieve. This card can cancel the effects of any Combat card, and the only card that can stop it is itself. Given that fact, the odds of it being stopped are really low.

3. Breakthrough Drill

Up until the release of the Trunks Saga, Stasis Decks were everywhere and dominated the environment. This card was one of the few weapons the players could use against Dragon Ball Decks. If you could keep your opponent from ending Combat, the game was yours. This card changed the environment and now a lot of the games are determined by it. The Breakthrough Drill shows you that there's always a way to fight a dominant deck.

4. Where There's Life There's Hope

This card falls in every deck. There's no reason a player wouldn't play it. Who can say no to keeping your opponent from winning when he thought he had already defeated you? This Non-Combat card sits in play until your opponent wins the game then it says "no, you have to wait one more turn." This card keeps your opponent from winning until the beginning of his next turn. It should be treated as your last chance to make a comeback and defeat your opponent.

5. Black Water Confusion Drill

This card was Score's answer to the players who were tired of losing to Dragon Ball Decks. The Trunks Saga has a lot of cards to fight Stasis Dragon Ball Decks and many ways to slow them down. This drill brought Beatdown Decks back, because while it's in play, no one can play Dragon Balls. If you're opponent is using a Dragon Ball Deck, he needs to find a way to deal with this drill before his Life Deck was gone. Some players argue that Score made a statement in the Trunks Saga that it doesn't like Dragon Ball Decks.

6. Black Style Mastery

The Black Mastery was the return of Beatdown Decks. This Mastery is nothing more than a drill that stays in play the entire game and improves all of your attacks to deal more damage. If you play a Black styled attack, it deals +2 power stages and +4 Life Card of Damage. With this card, all of your attacks can do an extra +4. When combined with big Physical and Energy attacks, it deals a ton of Life Cards of Damage.

7. Namek Dragon Ball 4

In the Trunks Saga, we get a new set of Dragon Balls and once again one of them stands out among the rest. Namek Dragon Ball 4's power allows you to discard all of your opponent's Non-Combat cards in play. With so many set-up decks in the environment, the Namek Dragon Ball 4 usually means game over and thanks for playing. The only major drawback of this Dragon Ball is if your opponent captures it, they make you discard all of your Non-Combat cards. Despite this concern, it's a risk worth taking.

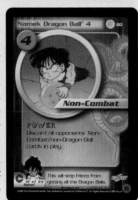

8. Red Style Mastery

This is the 2nd best Mastery in the set. It introduced a deck archetype that dominated the environment until the release of the Androids Saga. This Mastery provides the ability to gain two anger every turn by removing a card from your discard pile from the game. A small price to pay to be able to win in less than seven turns.

9. Android 20 Absorbing Drill

This drill is one of the cards that keeps players complaining. With this drill in play, you can stop any Energy attack by simply discarding two Life Cards. It's a really powerful card that can destroy your opponent if he's trying to beat you down with Energy attacks. This card is so powerful that I wouldn't be surprised if it were restricted in the near future.

10. Hero's Way

Here's the sleeper of the set. This card has so much potential and so much power it's not even funny. It can crush just about any Namekian Deck and it stops all of those decks that try to combo off their discard pile. The cool thing about it is if you're trying to set up your discard pile, this card is the best way to get rid of all the stuff you don't need. The ability to remove both discard piles from the game is a lot better than you can imagine.

Androids Saga

1. Android 18's Stare Down

It was cards like this one that allowed the villains to take over the tournament scene when the Androids Saga was released. No one can resist a card that allows you to look at your opponent's hand and make him discard any card. If you're using Android 18 as your main personality, you get to draw an extra card every turn and you can use up to four copies of this card. It gives you the hand advantage you need to take out your opponent.

2. Cell's Threatening Position C6

Tired of Anger Decks? Do you wish there was a way you could stop them once and for all? You'll find what you are looking for in this card. You'll be able to make your opponent go back to square one. This villain's only card allows you to set your opponent's Main Personality to level one. Wait for your opponent to get to his level four and use this card to set him back to level one. It'll take him too long to recover and give you enough time to take him out.

3. City in Turmoil

Say hello to the Battleground you'll find in most Survival Decks. This card turns off all Non-Combat cards in play and makes sure nobody can use them for the remainder of the game. The big drawback is that it will also turn off your Non-Combat cards. However, if you're using a pure Beatdown Deck, you shouldn't have many Non-Combat cards in play.

4. Piccolo the Trained Lv. 1

This card is the best personality the Android Saga has to offer. He has decent power stages and a power that will crush your opponent's strategy in seconds. Piccolo's personality power turns off your opponent's Main Personality power and doesn't let them use it for the remainder of the turn. Your opponent won't know what to do without it because his deck is built on being able to use personality power.

5. Blue Terror

This Energy attack is like having two cards in one. When you play it, you can search your Life Deck for any card and place it in your hand. It's ability to let you get any card you need at any given time makes this card almost broken. Cards that allow you to tutor for any other cards in your Life Deck are a welcome addition. The fact that this tutor can deal three Life cards to your opponent is just an added bonus.

6. Black Searching Technique

This card is so good I don't even know where to begin. The card deals two unblockable Life cards of Damage to your opponent, it allows you to look through your opponent's Life Deck, and you can remove any two cards you want from the game. It's not even limited to one per deck so you can pack three of them and pick your opponent's Life Deck. If you want, this card lets you get rid of all the blocks he has left and throw every attack you have at him.

7. Orange Stare Down

Once again we see how much Non-Combats hate what the Android Saga brought to the game. This card doesn't only remove Non-Combats in play from the game, but it's also an Energy attack. When combined with the Trunks Saga or Cell Saga Masteries it can capture a Dragon Ball. What more could you ask for when facing a Dragon Ball Deck? With this card you could remove their Goku's Capturing Drill and steal their Dragon Ball while you're at it.

8. Saiyan Inspection

Here's the sleeper of the set. Every set has a sleeper card that only gets better as time goes on. This card is like having an off switch to your opponent's personality card power. The only drawback is that after the release of World Games, there's a Sensei card that can nuke any Non-Combat cards in play. We all know how easy it is to deal with Non-Combat cards, but cards like this one are still worth using. You'll know what I mean when your opponent loses control of the game because he can't use his personality card power.

9. Namekian teamwork

Here's the new card Ally Decks received in the Android Saga. This card is the most recent button to nuke all of your opponent's Non-Combat cards in play. The catch is that you need to have in ally in play in order to use this card. If you're already using an Ally Deck, that shouldn't be a problem. The good thing is you don't have to discard any of your Non-Combat cards when you play it because you could lose board control.

10. Severe Bruises 112

I know most of you are wondering what this card is doing in the top 10 right? Well, if you're using a hero as your main personality, you can't use Cell's Threatening Position. But you still need to find a way to fight anger. This Non-Combat card is the best Terrible Wounds variant in the Android Saga. Not many Anger Decks use a lot of drills, so this card should be able to keep your opponents from gaining any more anger. In the meantime, you can focus on taking them out.

Cell Saga

1. Android 18 Lv. 1

This card has been dominating the environment ever since it was released. Her power allows you to set up your hand before you even draw it, plus you get to draw a card. Being able to look at the top six cards of your Life Deck and place them back in any order before you enter Combat is extremely powerful. When you add the ability to draw a card to it, it makes this card so much more appealing. The second reason why this personality is used by every gamer is the fact that she's Android 18. It's just amazing how silly kids can be nowadays.

2. Blue Style Mastery

Before the Cell Saga was released, the player base was asking for a good, playable Blue Style Mastery. This Mastery has a lot of potential because it turns any card in your hand into a Physical or Energy block that can lower your opponent's anger two anger levels. Having this Mastery in play is like having a block in your hand every time you enter Combat. Many say a good defense is a good offense. This card will prove them wrong.

3. Z Warriors Gather

Here's the mother of all ally tutors. This card doesn't let you use one or two allies and bring them into play. With this card, you can get up to seven allies in play at three power stages above zero. It easily translates into having seven extra cards you can attack and use to defend while your opponent only has his one Main Personality. If you can get this card into play at turn one, the game will be over before you know it.

4. Cell's Presence

Cell's Presence is one of the best ways to deal with Ally Decks, and it gives heroes a decent card instead of having to use The Plan. What makes this card playable is the current environment. If it wasn't for the card Z Warriors Gather, this card wouldn't be that great. It is just a card that has a lot of power and can be really strong when it needs it to counter an even stronger card.

5. Vegeta the Last Prince Lv. 3 HT

This has to be the best card ever made when entering Combat power. Nothing can top it. It allows you to look at your opponent's hand and make him discard any card when entering Combat. With this guy on your side, you'll always know what your opponent is planning and you'll be able to force him to discard the best card in his hand. You can't ask for anything more from a card.

6. Namekian Energy Focus

This Namekian card both turns itself into any Energy Combat card and lets you draw the bottom card of your discard pile at the same time. It is one of the few cards that will allow you to get two more cards in your hand. When used in the right deck, it can turn itself into an attack and become any Energy Combat card you might need at that time. Try it out with Pikkon in a Beatdown Deck. You'll see how strong this card can be.

7. Orange Energy Discharge

As far as Energy attacks go, this is the closest thing you can get to a Krillin's Heat Seeking Blast. This Energy attack might not be unblockable, but it hits for at least six Life cards of Damage. You can capture a Dragon Ball even if you don't have other modifiers in play. It also gets around two of the best cards that can stop Physical and Energy attacks: Yamcha's Skilful Defense and Goku's Super Saiyan Blast.

8. Orange Haulting Drill

I know what you're thinking and the answer is no, the editor didn't make a mistake and misspell the title of the card. This card was actually misspelled by Score and it's one of the mistakes that has never been fixed. However, spelling aside, this card is fairly decent. It can help you deal with Physical Beatdown Decks by minimizing the amount of damage you take from Physical attacks. While you have this drill in play you'll never take more than three power stages from a single Physical attack your opponent performs.

9. Krillin's Solar Flare

Krillin's Solar Flare is one of those cards that works well in theory. You might want to call this card a small Tapkar. The perfect set-up for it is a Saiyan Physical Beatdown Deck. When it's successful, your opponent can't play any Physical Combat cards for the remainder of Combat. Once you actually play the card, you realize that since your deck is packed with Physical attacks, your opponent will always have an Energy block in his hand. The only reason this card made the list is because it works well in a Backlash Deck.

10. Stunned

Every time a new set comes out, all the players must get together to pick the one card about which they are going to complain. The card for the Cell Saga has to be Stunned. This card causes a lot of players to never want to use Trunks, Piccolo and Krillin. Stunned is a strong card because it can win you the game when you face certain personalities. The rest of the time, it's a dead card that sits in your deck. Before you decide to use it, make sure there are players using those characters in your local area.

Cell Games

1. Straining Rebirth Move

It's not always how powerful a card is or how much damage a card can deal that makes it one of the best cards in the set. This is one of those cards. It's worded a little different than most cards for a very special reason. IQ's (me) daughter was born on 5/9/01 and that handsome devil just had to work those numbers into a card power. This card is the result of many hours of re-wording and playing around with card effects. Hope you like it.

2. Gohan's kick

This card changed the tournament environment for good. Dragon Ball Decks fear this card. Even some of the Survival Decks have to watch for it because once this card has been played, Combat will not end until both players can't do anything else. This card keeps your opponent from playing a card that can end Combat or cards that can mass block all the attacks you perform. It will also stop you from doing the same things, but if all you have in mind is beatdown, it turns out to be a pretty good trade off.

3. Caught Off Guard Drill

If this card wasn't heroes only, it would probably be the strongest card in the set. This drill allows you to name any card that cannot be played or used as long as the drill stays in play. It is the best way to deal with cards that can hurt you or cost you the game. With this drill in play, your opponent won't even be able to play those cards. You have to know what cards your opponent is using, and make sure you don't hurt yourself when you name a specific card.

4. Power of the Dragon

Expect to see Power of the Dragon repeatedly played until Score bans all Dragon Balls ever made. This card is the equivalent of Cell's Threatening when facing Dragon Ball Decks. It can be the game breaker because if you're opponent can't recover quickly, it'll be too late. There are a lot of cards that hurt Dragon Ball Decks but nothing like this card. Just don't waste it early or it may cost you the game.

DBZ CCG Top 10 Lists

5. Aura Clash

Ever since the game was released, there was a small flaw in it. The problem was that the main personality would always stay on his level one if he wasn't trying to win by anger. When this card hit the scene, it quickly changed the game because you were finally able to force your opponent to go to his level two. This meant that players could no longer make decks based on their level one alone. Aura Clash may have brought disruption to the environment, but it also allowed you to use your level two or level three powers, even if you weren't trying to win by anger.

6. Cosmic Backlash

As I've stated before, every time a new set is released, the players complain about a new card. When this card was released, it was considered the new broken card that would kill the game. Similar to the way that Android 18 was supposed to kill the game in Cell Saga. Cosmic Backlash was designed to help players fight Dragon Ball Decks because they were taking over the environment. It worked like a charm. A deck was finally built around this card and it completely crushed Dragon Ball Decks. It was also able to take down other decks that didn't rely on the Dragon Ball victory.

7. Goku's Dragon Ball Quest

How about a Dragon Ball Deck fast enough to race Anger Decks without having to end Combat? This card gave the Dende Dragon Ball Decks a huge boost in speed and allowed them to combo a lot easier. When this card is used correctly, it can win the game in a matter of turns without your opponent being able to stop you.

8. Dragon's Victory

This is one of the two new victory conditions Cell Games brought to the table. It may not have seemed like a great thing at first, but it was later used in different decks. Anger Decks started using it and it eventually became a deck of its own. Those decks are still being used today. This card has a lot of potential because it can be splashed into other decks to surprise your opponent. It also changed the Tuff Enuff environment because anger didn't matter before, but now you need to keep it in mind while building your deck.

9. Namekian Quick Blast

This card has to be the best focused attack ever made. It deals enough damage to allow you to steal a Dragon Ball, and you can recover any two cards while setting up your discard pile. It is a must for every Namekian Deck. Not only can it recover itself, but it's one of the best Energy attacks the Namekian Style has to offer.

10. Goku's Farewell

This is just one of those cards that are fun to use. With this card, you can surprise your opponent and he won't know what to expect. It allows you to go to your highest personality level, so you can beatdown your opponent with your super high power stages. However, be careful, because once you use this card you only have five turns to win the game. As the old saying goes, with great power always comes a great drawback.

World Games

1. Goku's Blinding Strike

This huge Energy attack is a must in almost every deck. It can hit your opponent's Life Deck for a lot of damage and get rid of his best cards. It's a Sensei only card that can hit your opponent for a total of seven Life Cards. If it's successful, you get to name any three cards and force your opponent to search his Life Deck and remove them from the game. You just can't go wrong with this card. It is one of the few playable Sensei Deck cards so always make room for it.

2. West Kai Sensei

West Kai Sensei is another card that can easily fall into any deck. This card can remove any two Non-Combat cards in play from the game during your attacker attacks phase. If your opponent has a Vegeta's Quickness Drill in play that's been hurting you or any other Non-Combat card, you can deal with them by using this card. The beauty of it is that it's a Sensei, which means you get to start the game with it in play. Non-Combat cards will not be able to harm you while you have this Sensei on the table.

3. Hero's Drill

This card is what many players are calling Dragon Ball hate 101. This drill gives Physical Beatdown Decks a chance when facing those annoying Dragon Ball Decks. While you have this drill in play, all of your successful Physical attacks can remove the bottom card of your opponent's discard pile. If any of your opponent's Dragon Balls are at the bottom of his Life Deck, you'll be able to remove them from the game. You may keep him from winning with this card alone.

4. Orange Style Mastery

Here's a brand new deck archtype waiting to happen. Orange has always focused on Energy beatdown in the past, but things have changed thanks to this Mastery. When it is combined with Cell HT level one, you get two Physical attacks doing +5 power stages of damage every turn. It can only get bigger when you perform more Physical attacks. Expect to see this Mastery in your local tournament scene. Be wary of the

power of this Mastery, with it your opponent can take you out in one turn.

5. Krillin, the Great

Krillin's Heat Seeking Blast anyone? Krillin has gone from a level three to the best personality level in the World Games Saga. His level three Constant Combat Power makes all of your Energy attacks do tons of damage. When you combine it with Energy attacks, it can't be stopped. What you have created for yourself is a killing machine. Expect this guy to take over the Florida environment, because you never know what'll come out of the Bag of Beans.

6. Namekian Style Mastery

This Mastery looks a lot like the Saiyan Saga Mastery from the Cell Saga, but there's a hidden deck archtype it brings to the table. Dragon Ball Decks have taken a huge hit in the World Games Saga which is why this Mastery was created. With it you get to draw the bottom card of your discard pile when entering Combat. When in play, you'll be able to recover the Dragon Balls placed at the bottom of your Life Deck in no time.

7. Energy Drain

This card is a small preview of how strong the Majins will be once the new set is released. We have already seen how strong Majin Vegeta's level one is, and how much potential there is when you combine him with this card. This card might bring back the Saiyan Lockdown Deck, because if you can keep your opponent at zero power stages, they won't be able to do anything.

8. Free Style Mastery

This Mastery is one of the craziest cards ever released. It allows you to tear apart your opponent's Life Deck without him being able to do anything, but you have to build your deck around this card alone. Goku the Puppet can be a lot of help when building the deck and there is so much you can do with this card. Try it out and you'll see what I mean.

9. Red Heat Seeking Blast

Every Style has a way to hurt Dragon Ball Decks and, for once, Red didn't get stuck with the worst card. This Energy attack will tear apart all the Blue Dragon Ball Android 18 Decks because they can't deal with this card. If you get one off against a Blue Dragon Ball Deck, it should be enough to finish it off. We're talking about a Focused Energy attack that can deal eight to ten Life Cards of Damage.

10. Goku's Quickness Drill

This card is the best metagame card in the set. It will take out the annoying Tapkar Backlash Decks that cause so many complaints. Whenever your opponent forces you to discard a card, Goku's Quickness Drill allows you to draw a card for every card you were forced to discard. You just can't go wrong with it. Even if it's discarded from your hand, you get to place it into play instead of discarding it.

Babidi

1- Daughter's Joy

I can imagine the look on most players' faces when they see this as the number one card in the set. And all I can say is "I'm writing this article, so I can pick what falls where and there's nothing you can do about it. MUWHAHAHAH!!!"

If you really have no idea why this card is even made, it's because one of Score's Game Developers likes to sneak in special dates and other details into the cards. In this case the numbers 5, 9 and 2 stand for 5/9/02, which is Megan's (my daughter's) second birthday.

The only other thing you should know about this card is that it's impossible to get one signed by the designer.

2- Blue Energy Dive

Have you ever wished you could get back your Cosmic Backlash, Dragon's Victory or maybe even your Goku's Dragon Ball Quest? Well, here you go! This card is good in Survival Decks, but even better in Combo Decks. The ability to be able to grab any two cards from your discard pile and place them on top of your deck can turn the tide of a game in a matter of seconds. If only this card was Styleless…

3- Initiative

This card was one of the first "problem" cards Score had to deal with once the Babidi Saga was released. This Non-Combat card was everything Dragon Ball Decks ever wanted. It allowed you to end combat before your opponent could play a Gohan's Kick that cost you the game. Even though you can only pack one in your deck, it's still as good as ever. Try it out and see for yourself… you won't be disappointed.

4- Red Sniping Shot

I know what most of you are thinking, and this card didn't make the list just because it can gain you 2 anger. Before you go online and tell the world that you can't believe IQ feels that Red Sniping Shot is better than Black Pivot Kick, think about the potential of this card.

Imagine the wonders it can do for an Ally Deck. It doesn't only sink your Main Personality 4 power stages, but it also makes

your opponent use two blocks or take 10 Life Cards. Although it's still good in Anger, it's even better in Ally Decks.

5- Black Pivot Kick

This Physical Attack is one of the good Sensei Deck Only cards that each style received. Although it's only a Physical Attack doing +3 power stages, it's the Secondary Effect that makes this card more playable.

Are you tired of your opponent locking you down with Drills or with pesky Allies who keep taking cheap shots at you? Why worry about them when you can nuke two of them with this single attack, while hitting your opponent for a decent amount of Life Cards? Just trust me when I say you'll be glad to be using this card in those situations.

6- Majin Vegeta (Lv. 1 Ultra rare)

How did Majin Vegeta manage to get in the top 10? Well, he has one of the best powers as far as Main Personalities go. His power not only allows you to hit your opponent for at least 5 Life Cards, but he also lets you gain power stages every time you play a card with Majin in the title. Everyone who's ever been locked down at 0 by a Physical Beatdown deck knows how great that power can be in play. Besides it gets even better if you are using Cell's Arena.

7- Orange Temple Strike

Orange Physical Beatdown Decks got two good cards in the Babidi Saga. One was this one and the other was Orange Rapid Attack. It took me a while to figure out which of the two cards should make the top 10. I had to go with this attack because it's not only great for Orange Physical Beatdown Decks, but it's also works well in a Styleless Deck.

Granted, it will most likely be replaced in Styleless decks once Namekian Sh... never mind, I shouldn't be talking about a card in the un-released Sagas.

8- Blue Trapped Strike

Here it is ladies and gentlemen, IQ's pick for the sleeper card of the set. I believe this Physical Attack has a lot of potential and it won't take long before the player base figures it out. This attack can easily be a game breaker in the Styleless Combo Anger Deck and it will be one of the strongest cards once the Majin Buu Saga is released. Just keep an eye on this card and you'll see what I'm talking about.

9- Hercule's Close Save

I can't remember the last time Score released a card that helped Dragon Ball Decks and also kept Combo Decks alive. This Non-Combat card is one of the few Score has released in a long time. It was one of the biggest bombs at the outset, but that quickly changed when it was limited to one per deck during playtesting.

Even though you can only use one copy of this card in your deck, it still has the potential to give you that extra turn you need to win the game. For this reason alone, it's worth being the 9th best card in the set.

10. Majin Power Drill

This card has made the list for two reasons. First, once the Buu Saga is released there will be more Majin Decks and this card is nasty with some of the attacks out there. The other reason is because Focused Attacks are usually game breakers. By having a card in your deck that makes every attack Focused, it becomes more than what a lot of decks can handle.

Promos

1. Trunks HT 1

This card took over the tournament environment when it was released back in the Trunks Saga and it's still going strong. Trunk's level one Constant Combat Power turns all of your opponent's Energy attacks into Energy attacks for two Life Cards of Damage. Once you have this guy in play, you take a maximum of two Life Cards from any Energy attack your opponent performs. It is great for a Dragon Ball Deck, because your opponent will never be able to capture your Dragon Balls.

2. HUH???

This Non-Combat card was just released in the World Games Saga and it's already a staple. A staple is a card that you have to play in your deck irregardless of what type of deck you use. What makes this card a staple is that it can remove a Dragon Ball in play from the game, and it's the best way to deal with Dragon Ball Decks. What makes the card even better is that it's a Sensei Deck Only card. If you know your opponent is not using a Dragon Ball Deck, you don't even have to put it in your deck.

3. Fatherly Advice

This card is the best tutor in the game. With it you can get almost any card from your discard pile or from your Life Deck. What makes it even better is that it's a Non-combat card, so you can let it sit there until you really need a card to stay alive or finish off your opponent. Having this card in play is like having any card at will. How can you go wrong with a card like this one?

4. Confrontation

This is one of the few playable heroes only cards ever made. It is a weaker version of the Android 18 Stare Down, but in the end it still gets rid of a card from your opponent's hand. Once played, you get to look at your opponent's hand and force him to shuffle a card back into his Life Deck. He may still draw the same card later in the game, but if you're trying to get rid of your opponent's blocks in order to hit him with your big attacks, this card is all you need.

5. Cell HT Lv. 1

This guy has been used and abused ever since he was introduced. He works well with the Black Trunks Saga Mastery and with the World Games Orange Style Mastery because his power allows you to perform two Physical attacks doing +3 power stages of damage. When you combine it with either one of the Masteries, his power can do insane amounts of damage. You can also try him in a Saiyan Lockdown Deck, because his power will help you keep your opponent's Main Personality at zero power stages.

6. King Kai's New Home

This Location only made the list because of the current environment. With this card in play, you can completely shut down any Tapkar Deck or any other deck that relies on heavy card drawing. This Location doesn't let a player draw more cards once that player has four cards in his hand. It can save you from those decks that try to build up a huge hand to overwhelm you.

7. Foreboding Evidence

Foreboding Evidence is another really good and strong card for villains. With this card, any villain can shuffle all the Combat cards in his discard pile back into his Life Deck. It's like starting the game all over again, because if you do it at the right time, you can get about twenty cards back into your Life Deck. If you like to use combo decks, use this card with a hero as your Main Personality. You'll be able to take any three cards from your discard pile and place them in any order on top of your Life Deck. This card is similar to an Earth Dragon Ball Seven only smaller.

8. Emotional Baggage

This card didn't make the list because of how strong it is or for how it can be abused in a certain combo. This card made the list just because I've been wondering if it really is the worst promo card ever made. After thinking for hours and hours, I can't come up a worse one. What makes this card awful is that only Vegeta can use it, if he has Trunks in play as an ally and your opponent discards him or removes him from the game. I'd rather use a Physical attack doing +1 power stage than this card. It's useless.

9. Team Work Kamehameha

Who wouldn't want to be using an Energy attack that does ten Life Cards of Damage? This attack deals a lot of Life cards of Damage to your opponent and your Main personality doesn't even have to pay any power stages. You do need to have an ally in play with at least four power stages, but that's not as hard as it sounds.

10. Gohan's Nimbus Cloud

There's no good reason why you wouldn't want to play this card. When you play it, you get to draw a card and there's nothing your opponent can do to stop it. You also get to search your Life Deck for a Location and place it in play. You're actually getting two cards from your deck with one card. If you ask me, that's a pretty good deal. ★

The 20 most collectible cards in the DBZ CCG

— BY ISRAEL QUIROZ

1) Champion Aura

This is currently the rarest card in the game, but there is only one available and it was given to the DBZ 2002 World Champion. Last I heard, the card sold on eBay for over $800 dollars and the owner is holding on to it. Don't expect to see this baby on eBay anytime soon. It's obvious why this card is so rare, and that's why owning this beauty is every collector's dream.

2) Victorious Drill

If you missed the 2003 DBZ World Championships, you also missed your chance at this card. This Drill was the prize for the top 64 players, and it's the second rarest card the game has to offer. It is considered a must in every deck and you won't find any for sale, which drives its value through the roof.

3) Champion Drill

This card was awarded to the first DBZ World Champion and was supposed to be unique, but a printing error allowed nearly 50 copies of this card to leak into Limited Android Saga booster packs. This card was also given to the top 16 players of the 2003 Worlds Championship and even though a number of

copies of this card are available to the public, its playability makes owners want to hold on to it. This card sells for more than $250.

4) Irwin Toys Set

I'm sure most of you have seen or at least heard about the Irwin Toy cards. You're probably wondering how this set landed on the 4th spot on this list. Once you sit back and consider the odds and ratios, it is nearly impossible to get the entire set by buying the toys and praying to get the cards you need. Each toy costs at least $10, which turns them into $10 booster packs that contain one card. Given that

there are over 30 IR cards, do the math on what it takes to get the complete set.

5) Vegeta's Energy Focu

Score Entertainment has used this card for many different things. At first, it was used as a first place prize at special events. This card's rarity is almost as high as the "Judge" and "Volunteer Only" cards. The card's playability and rarity makes it a must for players and collectors. No one knows whether Score Entertainment will ever make this card available to the open market through a specific promotion. Until then, Vegeta's Energy Force remains a highly prized wild card. Have fun trying to get it from one from the players who own it.

6) Gohan's Power Hit

Volunteers will be jumping through hoops to earn this card. It is Score Entertainment's brand new "Volunteer Only" card. Some say the "Volunteer Only" cards are the hardest ones to find because you never know who Score Entertainment might contact and draft for one of their events. Currently, there are a limited amount of these cards on the market. They're going for a shiny nickel on eBay. You may want to get your hands on one while you still can, because it's believed that there weren't many printed and once Score runs out, they will not be reprinted.

7) Blue Back Breaker

Score Entertainment's "Judges" have a new card they'll be trying to earn, and one can only imagine how much this card will be worth. Judge cards are worth a lot on the secondary market, and they are desired by players and collectors because of their playability.

A judge has to run a certain number of events

before he earns enough points to be rewarded with this card. It makes this card hard for collectors to find and rather valuable to the judges. Hopefully, there'll be more of these cards on the market because the number of judges keeps increasing. Whether they'll be willing to give up this card is a different story.

8) Namekian Strike

Namekian Strike was originally created for the Collector's Club, but the Collector's Club never materialized. If these cards didn't leak into the Limited Edition Android Saga booster packs by mistake, this card wouldn't be on the market. As far as I know, Score Entertainment is planning to release this card through a special collector's edition promotion in the near future. If that idea isn't approved, like the Collector's Club, then this card may never be officially released.

9) Black King Kai Set

This is a special set that was and is still only available to judges. They can earn these three cards by running events and volunteering at special Regional and National events. The set is hard to find because by the time a judge finally earns the entire set, they're not willing to sell it. It is nearly impossible for a collector to get his hands on the entire set.

10) Fatherly Advice

This is the first card that was made available only to judges. It was one of the rarest cards when it was released, but now it's rather easy to find for the right prize. The increase in the number of judges has made it easier for this card to get to the public. They are in limited supply, because Score Entertainment makes new judge cards instead of reprinting previous ones and decreasing their value. I don't think it'll be long before Score runs out of their supply, and once the demand for this card increases, it'll be difficult to find.

11) Limited Frieza, the Master

Frieza, the Master is one of the Ultra Rares from the Frieza Saga. Not many collectors have this card, because unless you were collecting from the beginning, you've never heard of this card. What makes it hard to find, is the fact that the game was new when the Frieza Saga was released and there wasn't a lot of product printed at the time.

12) Goku's Blinding Strike

Goku's Blinding Strike is the rarest card of the World Games Ultra Rares. Goku's Blinding Strike is also the most playable of the World Games Ultra Rares, which makes it a chase car for collectors and players alike. Expect this card to continue to be hard to find, because each player will want to have at least three copies of this card.

13) Goku, the Galaxy's Hero

This is the most recent Goku Level 5 Ultra Rare Personality card, and considering the value of previous Goku Personality Ultra Rare cards in the past,

this card will sell for a lot. I don't know why, but almost every time there's a Goku Personality Ultra rare card in the set, it's always the Ultra Rare that sells for more than the others. Maybe there's something about Goku that reaches out to people and makes them want to empty their wallets.

14) Pikkon the Prized fighter

This is the only card I'm not sure whether it belongs on the list. I feel it belongs because it's the only Pikkon Level 5 card ever made. Pikkon doesn't appear in the storyline after the World Games Saga. This fact may also be why collectors don't want this card. I guess it's up to the collectors and what they're collecting. If you're a collector who

wants every Ultra Rare, than you'll want this card. However, if you only desire cards with the main and well-known characters of series on them, you might not want to chase this card.

15) Majin Vegeta level 1 (alternate foil)

The Babidi Saga was released a few months ago, and this Ultra Rare appears to be the chase card in the set. I could be wrong, but keeping in mind the number of collectors out there, it may hard to get your hands on this card. Granted, it's believed that the Ultra Rare ratio was increased in this Saga, but no one knows the

rarity of the Alternate Foil Ultra Rare. It could be as scarce as a normal Ultra Rare card, but it may be harder to find than the normal Ultra Rares. It's one of those questions that will only be answered in due time.

16) Victorious

Victorious was initially given to the top 16 players of the 2002 Worlds Championship, but later it was the prize for the top 16 players of the 2003 Regional tournaments. There were 12 different Regionals, and every player who made top 16 got a Victorious.

The card might have lost some value among the player base because it was a "common" prize, but it's not easy for a collector who doesn't play the game to get this card. It's very unlikely that Score Entertainment will ever reprint it or use it for a promotion. If you're a collector who doesn't play the game and wants this card, you might have to buy it online or find someone who's willing to trade it away. A player may not value this card, but you never know.

17) Burger King Promo Set

The Burger King Promo Set (BK Set) was one of the first, if not the first promotion, Score Entertainment ever made. This set of cards came with DBZ figures and were only available with a Kids Meal. The promotion ran for a limited time, and then was discontinued. Keep in mind that this promotion was part of the Saiyan Saga, and the game was not as popular as it is today, so the interest in these promotional cards wasn't as high and there are not many complete sets available.

18) Kraft Promo Set

A total of 10 Kraft DBZ Promo cards were released in Australia through a cross marketing campaign with KRAFT. The marketing campaign was probably something like: "If you're a gamer … you like cheese!" We don't know what Score Entertainment was trying to achieve with this promotion, but we do know that there are 10 pink promotional cards that can only be found in Australia… and online.

I've seen the sets go for $50 and I don't know if the price will be going up or down because you have to buy a lot of cheese to get the set. It's rumored that the cards will eventually be released in the US, but I doubt it. You'll either need to start ordering Australian cheese or say goodbye to this set of cards.

19) Black Lunge

Black Lunge went from being a common card to one of the hardest cards to find. It was given to any player who showed up at Score Entertainment events last year, and then either Score ran out of them or they decided to stop giving them away. The card isn't valuable to players because it's not very playable. It's rather common to players. Given the lack of player interest, it's hard to find this card on eBay and nearly impossible for a collector to find. It's ironic how a card that's practically worthless to a player can mean so much to a collector.

20) Goku, the Mighty

This personality card was an insert in the Shonen Jump magazine. It had its own template and was only released through the magazine. No one knows how many of these cards were made or if it will be inserted in another magazine. It's highly unlikely that this card will ever be re-released and it might become one of the rarest commons Score Entertainment has ever released. This is a telling example of how you can get a promo card in a magazine for under five dollars, and it turns out to be worth much more after the fact. ✪

Online
Resources

Looking for more advice? The Internet is a great way to get the latest information on the DBZ Collectible Card Game. Here are a handful of online sites that provide information to DBZ CCG gamers:

www.pojo.com

Hey, it's our site, and we're obviously going to plug it first. We've got a fun Card of the Day feature, where we look at different card in detail on Monday, Wednesday & Friday. There's also news, tips, killer decks, and more. Fans are encouraged to participate in submitting tips and talking on the message board.

www.dbzcardgame.com

This is the Official Dragon Ball Z CCG site. This is the place to get the latest news on tournaments and other upcoming events. They've got a great card library and Message Board.

www.dragonballz.com

We can't leave off the Official Dragon Ball Z site. This site is more for the anime, and has a great on line store. If you've never been here, it's worth a visit.

www.deck-zone.com

This site has a nice encyclopedia of CCG cards, and frequent updates.

www.fanaticsnetwork.com

A decent message board and news updates.

This book is not sponsored, endorsed or otherwise affiliated with any of the companies or products featured in this book. This is not an official publication.